Starbo

MW01033369

Cruise Ship Cozy
Mysteries Series Book 1

Hope Callaghan

hopecallaghan.com
Copyright © 2015
All rights reserved.

***** *****

Visit my website for new releases and

special offers: hopecallaghan.com

A special thank you to Wanda D. and Peggy H. for taking the time to read and review the first book in this series, Starboard Secrets, and offering all of the helpful advice.

Contents:

CAST OF CHARACTERS V

CHAPTER 1 1

CHAPTER 2...15

CHAPTER 3 33

CHAPTER 4 63

CHAPTER 5 72

CHAPTER 6..89

CHAPTER 7 100

CHAPTER 8 115

CHAPTER 9 131

CHAPTER 10..150

CHAPTER 11 158

CHAPTER 12 167

CHAPTER 13..190

CHAPTER 14 197

CHAPTER 15 207

CHAPTER 16 225

CHAPTER 17..237

CHAPTER 18..251

BOOKS IN THIS SERIES 261

MEET AUTHOR HOPE CALLAGHAN 263

APPLE CRISP RECIPE....................................265

Cast of Characters

Mildred Sanders. Mildred "Millie" Sanders, heartbroken after her husband left her for one of his clients, decides to take a position as assistant cruise director aboard the mega cruise ship, Siren of the Seas. From day one, she discovers she has a knack for solving mysteries, which is a good thing since some sort of crime is always being committed on the high seas.

Annette Delacroix. Director of Food and Beverage on board Siren of the Seas, Annette has a secret past and is the perfect accomplice in Millie's investigations. Annette is the "Jill of all Trades" and isn't afraid to roll up her sleeves and help out her friend in need.

Catherine "Cat" Wellington. Cat is the most cautious of the group of friends and prefers to help Millie from the sidelines. But when push comes to shove, Cat can be counted on to risk life and limb in the pursuit of justice.

Andrew "Andy" Walker. The Cruise Director onboard and Millie's boss, has a booming voice and speaks with a British accent.

Chapter 1

Mildred Sanders came to an abrupt halt. She lifted her head and stared at the side of the enormous cruise ship. The sea breeze blew bits of her shoulder length gray locks into her eyes. She tucked the wayward strands of hair behind her ear as her eyes slowly ran the length of the ship, taking in every small detail of what was now her new home.

She straightened her back and pulled her roundish, barely five-foot tall frame ramrod straight. Her knuckles turned white as she squeezed the handle of her suitcase and yanked it along behind her.

The sound of her sturdy, black pumps clicked in rhythm to the wheels on her luggage as she made her way down the sidewalk. The sound echoed off the side of a long, low building that stood sentinel in front of the massive ship.

Millie sucked in a breath and stepped inside the drab, gray building. To the right was a small line of people. *Other crew*, Millie decided. Her new family. All of them complete strangers - until today.

She made her way to the end of the line before fumbling in her purse for her reading glasses and the thick stack of papers she had brought with her. Millie had filled out the paperwork weeks ago and submitted it online. It seemed like an eternity ago.

When it was Millie's turn, she grabbed the handle of her suitcase and dragged it to the counter.

It was obvious the woman behind the counter had done this dozens of times. Probably hundreds. She gave Millie an encouraging smile and picked up the driver's license Millie had placed on the counter. She swiped the license through a scanner attached to the side of her computer monitor and handed it back.

The woman pointed to a round lens on the edge of the counter. "Look in the camera and smile."

With a few more clicks on her keyboard, the woman reached behind her and grabbed a card that had magically dropped from a whirring machine. She glanced at the photo and slid it across the counter in Millie's direction.

Millie picked it up and studied the picture. The look on her face reminded her of someone who had narrowly avoided the dreaded door-to-door insurance salesman. *Joy. She would be stuck with this horrible picture ID for a very long time.*

Millie picked up the lanyard and card, resisting the urge to toss it in the trash and beg the woman behind the counter for a do-over. She had a twenty-dollar bill in her pocket. *Maybe she could bribe her...*

"Thank you," Millie managed to croak.

The woman smiled reassuringly and pointed. "Just follow the arrows."

Millie's eyes dropped to the floor. She took a deep breath, grabbed the handle of her suitcase, and began the final steps to her new life. There was no turning back now.

She followed the arrows until she reached the gangplank. For the tenth time that day and probably the millionth time in the last month, she wondered how on earth she had ended up here.

A sixty year-old mother and grandmother should know better than to make a semi-rash decision to leave the comforts of hearth and home and embark on a new career. Over a thousand miles from everything familiar, and of all places on a cruise ship.

She would like to think it was a thoughtless moment, an impulsive decision, but it really hadn't been. Mildred, or Millie as everyone called her, had tossed around the idea of a drastic change in her life for months now. Ever since Roger, her ex-husband, had dropped a bomb when he informed her he was moving out of their comfortable home in the suburbs and moving in with one of his clients. Delilah Osborne to be exact. Delilah also happened to be Millie's hairdresser.

When Roger first said the woman's name, Delilah, it hadn't registered. It took a day or two for the whole thing to sink in. By then, Roger had packed up what he wanted and moved out. The only things he had left behind were crap he didn't want.

It gave Millie a bit of pleasure the night she built a roaring bonfire in the backyard and burned every single thing that reminded her of him. Which was a lot.

Looking back, she should've realized the neighbors would call the fire department when the flames shot over ten feet in the air and torched a few of the leaves on the tree that hung over Millie's fence. How was she to know Roger's "mantique" collection of mounted deer antlers would burn that hot?

By the time the fire department arrived, Millie had doused the flames with the garden hose. She couldn't understand what the big deal was. Anyway, after that night, the house was a whole lot cleaner - and emptier.

Delilah Osborne had hired Roger, a private investigator, to track down her husband's investments. She was convinced her husband had a small fortune stashed in overseas bank accounts and she was right.

When the woman found out how much money her husband was hiding from her, she took him to the cleaners and walked away with a tidy amount of cash. Millions...Roger had told his wife.

Millie often wondered if the money was what had attracted Roger. For all thirty-eight years of their marriage, he had worked days, nights, and even weekends building their business*: Central Michigan Private Investigators.* Of course, it was really only "investigator" and that investigator was her husband, Roger.

Millie had been more of the behind-the-scenes partner while Roger did the nitty-gritty work. Covert operations, stakeouts, tailing people, exposing cheating spouses. Although sometimes Millie would tag along, but that was rare. Roger had always reminded her that investigating was a man's job.

She jerked her suitcase up and over the edge of the ramp. Just the thought of her ex-husband caused her blood pressure to spike a good ten points.

In the beginning, Millie felt crushed. She never saw it coming. Now she was glad. *The money-grubbers could have each other.*

Millie was still young. Still up for an adventure, which was why she was where she was at that moment. She had something to prove, not only to herself, but also to the world.

It had all worked out in the end. Roger and she had had a semi-amicable divorce. He kept the business. She got the house - which they had owned free and clear - and he signed over all of the retirement accounts. All two of them. Little did she know that he had "borrowed" from the accounts to fund his mid-life crisis, which included the disgusting taxidermy collection.

Still, Millie had enough money to live on. What she needed now was purpose in her life. When she saw the online ad for an assistant cruise director, it was like an answer to prayer. The ad had Millie's name written all over it.

"Come work for one of the largest, most prestigious cruise ship companies sailing the seas. Majestic Cruise Lines is searching for the needle in the haystack. A one-of-a-kind person who is adventurous, outgoing and creative, to join our team as assistant cruise director on our newer ship, the Siren of the Seas.

This position requires an eight-month commitment. For more information and an application, please contact us at the email address listed below."

No one had ever called her adventurous or outgoing, but she figured if she got a job on board a cruise ship that would certainly fit the bill. Before she could change her mind, Millie filled out the on-line application and sent it off.

A week passed and Millie had almost given up. Almost. The day she received a reply stating that the company was interested in doing a phone interview, Millie almost passed out.

Her heart raced as she dialed the number. The voice on the other end was warm and friendly. The interview had gone off without a hitch and Millie was certain she had passed the interview with flying colors.

When the company called back a week later and asked her to come to Miami for a face-to-face interview, Millie almost backed out. She didn't dare tell her son, Blake, or daughter, Beth that she was going. They would think she had lost her mind. Maybe she had, but the more she thought about it, the more convinced she became that God had shown her the ad.

Millie prayed about it and by the time she boarded the plane for Miami, she was at peace. If God meant for her to get this job, then she would get it.

The interview process consisted of talking to several employees in the personnel department. After finishing her third interview, the woman offered her the job on the spot and Millie accepted. She had three weeks to get her affairs in order back home before her contract began and the ship set sail.

The first thing she did when she arrived back home was call a family meeting. The look on her children's faces when she told them the news, was priceless. She wasn't far off when she thought they would think she had lost her mind, but all that was behind her now. Millie stepped over the threshold and inside the entrance to the ship.

Roger and she had been on a cruise not long before he left her and the ship they were on didn't resemble it in the least.

She looked around the glitzy, gleaming interior. The brass and glass atrium soared high above. A sea of voices bounced off the towering space and echoed around her. Off to the left was a set of glass elevators. To the right - a long counter. A cozy cluster of chairs dotted the spacious area.

Millie took a step toward the counter on the right when an anguished cry filled the air. Off to one side, near what looked to be a bar area, a small group of people had gathered...a group of uniformed crewmembers to be exact.

She grabbed the handle of her suitcase and inched closer to the commotion. Someone was lying on the floor. That someone was wearing bright purple stiletto heels.

"Then she just keeled over. R...right there in front of me," a young man explained to an older man wearing a white uniform. Both men were leaning over what Millie could now see was a woman's body.

The man in uniform pressed his fingers to her throat and shook his head. The older man in the white outfit stood abruptly. "She's gone."

Millie swallowed hard. Her eyes darted to the body lying on the floor. The woman's left arm was twisted at an odd angle while her other arm was splayed across her blue blazer. Toned, muscular legs thrust out below a matching blue skirt.

Her eyes traveled from the top of the woman's head to the tip of her high-heeled shoes. Despite the gravity of the situation, the first thought that popped into Millie's head was that if the woman worked for the cruise line, those shoes would be killer to wear all day.

The man in white was obviously the man in charge. He glanced around at the growing crowd, snapped his two-way radio from the clip attached to his belt and lifted it to his lips. "We need a stretcher and cover at the atrium bar ASAP!"

"Okay folks. The show is over." A burly man, wearing a light blue button-down shirt began waving his arms. "Time to get back to work."

Millie took a step back, her head spinning. She hadn't been on the cruise ship ten minutes and someone was already dead.

When she turned around, she ran smack dab into a man who was also wearing a white uniform, except the top of the man's sleeves had stripes. Uniform stripes, and he looked none too happy. "I'm sorry," Millie apologized as she backed away.

He gave a curt nod before sidestepping her. Millie took a quick glance back before heading to the stairs. She hadn't the slightest idea where to go from here.

Chapter 2

Millie wandered around aimlessly until she remembered the kind woman at the counter had given her a map. She fished it from her purse, slipped her glasses on and studied the ship's layout.

A young man stopped to help. "Are you looking for the crew quarters?"

Millie nodded. "Yes. I have no idea where I'm going."

The young man pointed to an elevator and a set of stairs. "Go down to deck two. When you reach deck two, you'll see another set of stairs. Go down one flight. Turn left and head straight out through the door that says "*Employees only.*"

Millie thanked him and headed to the stairs, repeating his instructions in her head. Her memory wasn't as sharp as it used to be. Unless, of course, it was something unimportant. Like remembering that Roger's favorite snack was trail mix - the one with coconut. Or that he liked his white socks on the left hand side of the dresser drawer and his black socks on the right.

She shook her head and scolded herself. *He has no business occupying real estate inside your brain.*

Eventually Millie found the door and stepped through. It was like entering a different world. The first thing that came to mind was that it was dark. Everything around her was a shade of drab gray.

She wrinkled her nose. Several stomach churning smells assailed her nostrils at the same time. The smell of stale cigarette smoke, rotting vegetables and sweat. Millie swallowed hard and forced herself to keep moving.

She found her way to the employee quarters and her assigned cabin. After inserting her brand new key card in the slot, she pushed the door open, flipped the light switch on and stepped inside.

Millie's heart sank. The room was small. The entire cabin was no larger than the back deck on her house.

She was still standing there trying to get over the shock when someone came crashing through the door behind her. The handle whacked Millie in the back, propelling her into the room and she lurched forward. Millie thrust her hand out to grab onto the edge of the bunk to steady herself.

"Oh my gosh. I am so sorry."

Millie kept one hand on the bed as she turned around. Standing behind her was a petite woman with jet-black hair and olive-colored skin. "Are you okay?"

Millie nodded. "I'm fine."

The young woman held out a slender hand. "You must be Mildred. I'm Sarah, your cabin mate."

Millie took her hand and shook it lightly. "Nice to meet you, dear," she said. "You can call me Millie."

The young woman's eyes glazed over as she looked over Millie's shoulder. "This room is **tiny**."

A set of bunk beds took up most of the small space. Across from the bunk beds was a half desk that had seen better days. Above that was a TV that looked to be about the same age as the desk. On the other side of the small desk was a door.

From where she was standing, Millie could open the door without taking a single step. In fact, she could touch the bunk beds with one hand and the door handle with the other.

She took a single step, pulled the door open and peered inside. It was a bathroom. She flipped on the light and blinked at the microscopic space.

Sarah peered over Millie's shoulder. "That is our bathroom?"

Millie started to chuckle, which made Sarah giggle. Soon, the two doubled over in laughter.

"Wait. Wait." Millie stepped into the closet-size bath, plopped down on the toilet lid and stretched out her arms.

Her fingertips touched the back wall of the shower and the mirror over the sink at the same time. "Great. We can save time by brushing our teeth and showering all at once," Millie joked.

Sarah wiped her eyes with the back of her hand. She looked back at the narrow bunk beds. "I'll take the top bunk if you don't mind."

Millie followed her gaze. The space between the top bunk and ceiling was tight. "Are you sure? I don't mind taking the top bunk..."

Sarah held up her hand. "I insist."

Millie wasn't looking for special treatment, but she wisely caved on this one. She was a bit on the claustrophobic side and the fact that one couldn't even sit upright in the top bunk without hitting their head wasn't lost on her.

She eyed the floor-to-ceiling closets near the door. "Tell you what...since you gave up the lower bunk, you get your pick of closets," Millie bargained.

Sarah smiled. "It's a deal." She stepped over to the closets and opened one of the doors. The closets were larger than they looked. She peered in the second closet. It was identical to the first one. "I'll take the one on the right."

Millie backed up and pulled out the small chair in front of the desk. "Why don't you unpack first?"

It didn't take long for Sarah to unload her small suitcase. She placed a pile of neatly folded clothes on the small shelf, and then hung the two dresses she'd brought with her on the hangers.

Sarah's friend, Nikki, had told Sarah to pack light. Since the crew wore uniforms, there was no sense in packing a bunch of extra clothes. They would have limited hours off, and the hours that they did have off would probably be spent sleeping. She was glad she had taken her friend's advice.

Nikki was on her second year contract on board the ship, the Siren of the Seas, and Sarah had hoped they would be sharing a cabin. At first, she was disappointed to have Millie as her roommate, but the more she thought about it, the more she realized this might work out better. Less partying, less drama.

Millie made small talk as she watched Sarah unpack. "So what will you be doing on board the ship?" she asked.

Sarah placed her tennis shoes on the closet floor and turned to Millie. "I'll be working in the dining room," she told her. "My friend, Nikki, works on this ship. She's the one that got me the job. What about you?"

Millie grabbed her small suitcase and shuffled over to the closet that was now hers. She unzipped the case and lifted the lid. "I'll be working as the assistant cruise director."

Millie caught the small lift of Sarah's eyebrows, and knew the young woman was surprised. She didn't look like she would be in charge of entertainment. In fact, she didn't look like she'd be the head of anything. She still wasn't 100% sure how she even got the job.

"That sounds like a fascinating job," Sarah admitted.

Millie pulled her few belongings from the suitcase and carefully placed them on the shelves.

She hung her two skirts and three blouses on the empty hangers. She had brought one pair of pumps, which she was wearing, a pair of navy blue sneakers and some black work shoes.

In the very bottom of the suitcase was a picture of her children and her. Her daughter, Beth, Beth's husband, David, and their two children - Millie's grandchildren - Noah and Bella. Also in the picture was her son, Blake, and of course, Millie.

She blinked back sudden tears. The last few weeks had been a whirlwind and reality was finally sinking in. She was about to embark on the adventure of a lifetime...an almost yearlong commitment to the high seas. Miles and miles away from her family and friends.

Sarah's heart went out to Millie as she gazed at the picture. She couldn't imagine leaving her family. She wondered what had happened that would make someone - especially someone her age - leave everything behind.

She watched as Millie carefully placed the picture frame in the corner of the small desk. "You have a lovely family," Sarah told her.

Millie eyed Sarah, who was now sitting on the edge of the lower bunk. "They think I'm crazy," she confessed as she smoothed the edge of her blouse and studied the photo.

Before Sarah could reply, there was a light tap on the cabin door.

Sarah made it from the bed to the door in four short strides. She opened it a crack and peered out. It was her friend, Nikki.

She swung the door open and Nikki stepped in. At first, the young woman didn't notice Millie. "Well. What do you think?"

Sarah scrunched up her nose. "I know you told me the room would be small but, this place is teeny."

24

"Don't worry. The only thing you'll be doing in here is sleeping and showering," she reassured her friend. "Have you met your cabin mate yet?"

Millie cleared her throat as Nikki peeked around Sarah's shoulder. "Oh, I'm sorry. I didn't see you."

Millie stepped forward and extended her hand. "I'm Mildred, but you can call me Millie," she told the young woman.

Nikki took her hand in a warm grip. "Nikki Tan." Her eyes studied Millie. It dawned on her that this was the new assistant cruise director. "I've heard all about you."

Good, I hope, Millie thought.

Nikki turned to Sarah. "The staff meeting starts at five down in the employee dining room," she explained as she glanced at her watch. "I can show you around if you'd like to see where the crew hangs out." She included Millie. "You can come, too."

There certainly wasn't much else to do and with three people in the cabin, the walls were starting to close in. "If you don't mind me tagging along."

Millie followed the young women into the hall. *I hope the entire crew on board isn't in their 20's or I'm going to stand out like a sore thumb,* she decided.

The three of them walked for what seemed like forever. The corridor stretched out as far as the eye could see.

"Welcome to what the crew nicknamed I-95. You know, like the highway," Nikki said.

They stopped in front of a set of large, glass doors.

"This is the crew mess," Nikki announced. It was the crew dining room. The place was bustling with activity. They stepped inside and made their way to the end of the buffet line.

Millie reached for an empty tray and scooted down the line. She grabbed a side salad, a sandwich and a small bag of potato chips. Nikki nodded to a few people she passed as she led the women to a table in the corner.

After setting her food on the table, Millie unfolded her napkin and plucked out a dinner fork. "Do you work in the dining room, too?"she asked Nikki.

Nikki lifted the top of her hamburger bun and squeezed a glob of catsup on the patty. She shook her head. "Nope. I work in guest services."

Millie twirled the straw inside the water glass. "That wouldn't be for me," she said. "You've probably heard it all."

"And then some," Nikki grinned. "The stories I could tell. So you're the new assistant CD."

Millie nodded as she opened her bag of potato chips and pulled one out. "I'm still not quite sure how I got the job."

"So what's my boss like?" Millie was more than a little curious about her new boss. She prayed that they would hit it off.

"Andrew Walker. You'll like him," Nikki told her.

Sarah plucked a fry from her plate and dipped it in the catsup. "Did you see the body they took out near the bar on deck five earlier?"

Millie scrunched her eyebrows and nodded. "It must've happened right before I got on."

Nikki set her burger on her plate. "I didn't see what happened, but it's all the buzz around here. Her name was Olivia LaShay. I heard she died."

Millie glanced down at the salad still on her plate. The thought of a dead person made her stomach churn.

Apparently, the idea of a dead person didn't bother Nikki. She pulled her piece of chocolate cream pie forward, picked up her fork and took a big bite. "She worked in the gift shop upstairs."

Nikki looked around and then leaned in. "Someone said she was poisoned."

Sarah paused, mid-bite. "Before she got on the ship?"

"I don't know. The details are kind of sketchy right now. No one seems to know and the big shots, they're keeping a tight lid on info so far, so it's pretty much just gossip at this point."

She turned to Millie. "I bet you could find out more since Andy was one of the first people on the scene when she collapsed."

Millie wondered if he had been the one waving people away. "What does he look like? Andy, I mean."

Nikki opened her arms. "He's about this wide and balding on top. He has a loud voice, like he's yelling all the time," she added.

Millie nodded. Andy *was* the man she had seen earlier. Her boss. "So you like him?"

Nikki nodded. "Yeah. From what I know. Of course, I don't know him all that well. He doesn't mingle much with the crew." She altered her voice and added a British accent. "I bloody well hope he's a decent chap for your sake."

Millie chuckled at the pathetic attempt. At least the cruise director was a little more...well, a little more mature. Closer to her own age. She wasn't sure how she would feel about working for someone who was younger than her children. "I guess I'll find out soon enough."

The women carried their dirty dishes to the side bin and emptied them in the large container. The staff meeting would begin shortly and Millie was getting a tad nervous. The more employees that wandered in, the more nervous she became.

The meeting was brief. It was apparent that quite a few of the staff was returning for a second contract. Millie was relieved that there was a good mix of age groups. Both younger and older, like herself. Of course, the younger was the majority and her age group the minority.

She was surprised to learn during the meeting that guests wouldn't be arriving until the next morning.

After the meeting ended, Millie headed back to the room to change into her official uniform, which consisted of a white shirt, navy blue blazer, and white polyester slacks. Her nametag was already pinned to the front.

She gave herself the once over in the mirror, took a deep breath and headed for the door. It was time for Millie to meet her new boss.

Chapter 3

Millie stepped into the corridor and glanced to the right then left, not exactly sure which way she should go. She watched as people darted here and there. They all seemed to know where they were going.

She slipped off to the side. *Where is the most likely place the cruise director would hang out?* Millie wondered. Then it dawned on her. She remembered her employee packet mentioned Vegas style and other shows on board every night that the cruise director and his assistant supervised. He was probably with the performers at the back of the stage.

She climbed the stairs to the first passenger level and wandered over to the bank of elevators to study the diagram on the wall - the ship layout.

If she was reading the diagram correctly, she was on the same side of the ship as the theater. All she had to do was climb two more levels.

Millie suffered from claustrophobia and a fear of elevators so she opted for the stairs. At the top of the landing, she headed to the side. To the right was a double set of metal doors. To the right of the doors hung a sign: *Theater*.

She opened the door and stepped inside. It was dark and the lights were off. Her eyes adjusted to the lack of light and she noticed that there was row after row of wide, padded seats. They seemed to go on forever.

Her eyes drifted upward. On the second level was another section of balcony seating.

She took a step forward. Several long aisles led to a large center stage. Directly in front of the stage was an orchestra pit.

Millie walked down the center aisle. She could hear muffled voices coming from somewhere behind the shimmering red velvet curtains that hung from the ceiling.

She spied a set of steps leading up the side of the stage. With a quick glance back, she quietly headed up the stairs and behind the stage.

A small, narrow doorway separated the side stage from the back. Bright lights beamed through the opening and the voices grew louder. Muffled laughter sounded from somewhere. *Laughter...a positive sign.*

She took a few more steps forward and *BAM*. A towering giant ran smack-dab into her. Like a charging bull.

"Ugh." All Millie could see were legs. Legs that were almost eye level. Well, perhaps not quite eye level. Maybe a little lower. More like her chin level.

Millie tilted her head back and looked at the young woman. If Millie had to guess, she was in her early twenties. Long, red fingernails grazed the top of Millie's arm as the woman released her hold. "I'm sorry. I didn't see you."

Millie smiled. *Yeah, probably because I look like an ant.* "It's really my fault for sneaking around back here," she assured the young woman.

Behind the blonde female Adonis was a cozy area, which reminded Millie of a large closet. Shimmering outfits lined the walls as far as the eye could see. The outfits were all color-coordinated. An array of tall hats with plumes of feathers sat on shelves above the garments, organized in the same meticulous manner as the outfits.

To the right of the wardrobe area, where the light was spilling out, were makeup counters. Long mirrors lined one wall. Bright bulbs beamed down on the counters. Plastic makeup cases and an

36

assortment of hairbrushes and combs took up nearly every inch of space.

The woman glanced at Millie's nametag. Her hand flew to her mouth. "You're the new assistant cruise director." Her hand shot out. "I'm Alison Coulter, one of the dancers."

Millie took the proffered hand as she studied the girl's face. Her bright blue eyes twinkled mischievously and her gleaming white smile made Millie want to smile in return, which she did.

Alison released her hold. "You must be looking for Andy."

Millie nodded. "The cruise director."

"Follow me." Alison spun around and began walking in the direction of the makeup room. Millie broke into a trot to keep pace.

They stepped into the bright room packed full of people. It reminded Millie of a can of sardines. Young, slender and fit sardines.

At the end of the crowded aisle, Millie spied the man she had seen earlier in the atrium. He was the same one who had been telling people to move off, away from the young woman's body that had been lying on the floor.

Andrew Walker must have felt eyes staring at him. He turned to face Millie. "Let me guess. Mildred Sanders." Now that she was close to him, she was able to get a good look at her new boss. He wasn't tall, but he was burly. Andrew Walker wasn't fat, but more thick and muscular.

His reddish hair was sparse and cropped, and he sported a moustache that matched the color of his hair. His thick, bushy eyebrows moved up and down when he talked. Millie's first thought was that it must tickle. He reminded her a bit of Yosemite Sam, except with less hair and less moustache.

38

His dark eyes narrowed - just a bit - as he studied Millie. That lasted for a fraction of a second. He flashed a big smile and a dimple appeared above the pencil-thin moustache.

Millie sucked in a breath as he cleared his throat. He thrust his hand out and began to pump hers as he talked. "Andrew. Andrew Walker. But you can call me Andy."

He pulled a handkerchief from his front pants pocket and dabbed at his thick brows. "The lights in here are cooking me alive." He shoved the handkerchief back in his pocket before continuing. "I am so glad you're here. I was going to track you down but…"

He paused, as if considering his next words carefully. "We had a small - err - unfortunate mishap down in the atrium earlier."

Millie nodded. "A terrible tragedy. I happened to stumble on the scene myself."

Heads in the room turned as others began to tune in to the conversation. Andy glanced around, and then nudged her elbow. "Let's step outside where it's cooler."

He led her out of the brightly lit room and into the large closet area, which was empty. The staff had congregated inside the claustrophobic area, as if they enjoyed being in tight quarters together. Millie made a mental note to avoid the area during peak times, if possible.

"C'mon. Follow me." Andy didn't wait for an answer as he headed down the steps and out of the theater. He abruptly stopped outside a door marked "Crew Only." With a twist of the handle, he opened the door and gave it a sharp push before stepping to the side and waiting for Millie to cross over the threshold.

The area reminded Millie of the deck where her cabin and other crew facilities were located. The only difference was this place was empty and it smelled better. The smell reminded her of fresh paint.

Their steps echoed on the gray metal floor as they walked. Millie wasn't sure if the subject was taboo, but she did wonder about the poor, unfortunate woman who had died. "Any idea what happened to that girl in the atrium?"

Andy gave her a sideways glance, but never changed pace. "They're still trying to sort it out." He looked ahead and then behind him as he lowered his voice. "It appears that she had been bitten by something."

He shook his head. "It left a nasty, ugly wound on her ankle." He lifted his hand and separated his thumb and forefinger. "It was a large, gaping sore about this big around."

Millie's brows furrowed. "Any idea what might have caused it?"

"Someone said it looked like a spider bite."

The thought hadn't occurred to Millie, but it made sense. Cruise ships traveled to islands. Islands with tropical forests and jungles. Jungles meant creepy crawlies. She decided right then and there to do a thorough inspection of her cabin and her bed.

Andy stopped abruptly. "Just between you and me, the young lady had been off the ship on break and had just gotten back on board for her next contract. I hope that means that whatever she got into, she got into whilst she was onshore."

That did little to ease Millie's mind. There was no guarantee that the woman hadn't been bitten on the ship. "What was her name?" She thought the girls had mentioned it earlier but couldn't remember what it was.

"Olivia LaShay. She worked in the gift shop." Andy went on. "Sweet enough girl, but she had a lot of drama and lots of different boyfriends that also worked on the ship. Olivia wasn't real popular with the other women, either. She made a game out of stealing their boyfriends and then dropping them like a hot potato when she got bored."

Millie perked up. Maybe someone had murdered her. Even though she had rarely been part of Roger's street investigations, she frequently helped him work on the different cases. He'd always said she had good gut instincts.

Andy opened another large, metal door. Millie was careful to step up and over the frame. She was so intent on making sure she didn't trip and fall, and make a fool of herself, she ran smack-dab into a tower of confection...a large tiered cake. She pulled her arm back, which was now sporting a thick layer of ocean blue creaminess.

Behind the towering creation were two piercing blue eyes that peered at her over the top of wire-rimmed glasses. Dark brown locks poked out from under a white hat.

"Will ya' look at that." The wisp of a woman slid the damaged goods onto the top of the stainless steel cabinet beside her and grabbed a clean dishrag from a nearby drawer.

She held the rag in one hand. Using her finger, she swiped at a mound of thick frosting still clinging to Millie's arm. She stuck the frosting-coated finger in her mouth. "Not bad, but it could use just a bit more sugar."

Without waiting for permission, she started to scrape the frosting from Millie's arm. "This cake is destined for the dumpster. Believe it or not, this is the second run in this cake has had with body parts. I won't tell you the other body part it made contact with." She winked. "Three strikes, and you're out." She made a thumbing motion.

Andy cleared his throat. "Not on my watch, Annette." He kept a close eye on the woman, who was still wiping the frosting off as he pushed the cake out of reach. "You know I need that cake in an hour for the captain's party."

"I know. I was just kidding. I'll fix 'er up in a jiff," she promised.

The woman dropped the frosted rag on the counter and crossed her arms. "I guess you're not going to introduce us. Some cruise director you are," she teased as she turned to Millie. "Annette Delacroix, Food and Beverage Manager, at your service."

Millie took her hand. She liked this woman. She seemed straightforward and to the point. It also didn't hurt that she appeared to be somewhat close to Millie's own age. "Mildred Sanders, Assistant Cruise Director." She released Annette's hand. "But you can call me Millie."

Annette's eyes crinkled in a warm greeting. She gave Andy a sideways glance. "About time you got someone decent over in your department."

45

Andy jerked back. "What was wrong with Toby?" he demanded.

Annette stuck her hand on her hip and locked eyes with Andy. "Nothing. As long as you could find him. When he wasn't hitting on every single female wearing a skirt." She turned back to Millie. "Toby didn't last long." She wagged her finger. "His biggest problem was fraternizing with the guests."

Annette picked up the damaged dessert and turned to go. "It was nice meeting you, Millie," she called over her shoulder. "If you need anything, you can almost always find me right here in the kitchen." With that, she rounded a corner and disappeared from sight.

Andy headed in the opposite direction. "Annette is a real gem. She's a little tough on the outside but a real softie on the inside."

The kitchen was huge and it wound around, back and forth, almost like a maze.

Millie nodded and waved at several of the staff who were hard at work prepping food. She followed him through a revolving door on the other side, which led into one of the dining rooms.

Several employees were setting tables, arranging flowers and wrapping silverware. Andy greeted several of the workers but never stopped.

They exited the double glass doors and entered a large, open area that overlooked the atrium.

Millie inched closer to the railing and peered down. Her eyes wandered to the bar area...to the spot where the woman's body had been just hours earlier.

The sound of music drifted up. Off to one side was a baby grand piano. Sitting at the keyboard was a woman. The tune she was playing was vaguely familiar.

Andy came up beside her. "Such a sad thing about that young woman," he commented as he

47

pointed to a spiral staircase. On the other side of the staircase was a long, gleaming counter. "We're headed over there."

Her boss picked up the pace as they strolled around the walkway and headed down the stairs. She followed him to the counter and to a man standing behind it. The man didn't look up. He was studying pages in a thick notebook. Every second or so, he would put a check mark next to something in the book.

Andy tapped lightly on the countertop. Finally, the man lifted his head. Millie grinned as she looked at his hair, which spiked out in every direction. If the spikes made contact at just the right angle, Millie was convinced they could poke an eye out.

"How are you doing, Donovan?"

The young man set his pen on top of the notebook. "Getting things in order." His eyes traveled from Andy to Millie. "Is this your new sidekick?"

"Yes." Andy shifted to the side. "Donovan Sweeney, this is Millie Sanders."

Donovan didn't offer his hand. Instead, he reached inside the drawer in front of him and pulled out a key card. He laid it on the counter and slid it in Millie's direction. "Welcome to the Siren, Millie." He tapped the tip of his finger on top of the card. "You'll need this," he told her.

She glanced at Donovan's tag before she picked up the card. On the front was her picture with the same deer-in-headlights, I'm-about-to-get-arrested look.

The card was colorful, unlike her room card, which was plain. A palm tree with waves lapping at the bottom was in the lower corner. She glanced over at Andy, her eyebrow raised.

"Don't lose that." He pointed to the card in her hand. "It gives you access to areas of the ship that other crew members don't have."

Donovan nodded. "Like the bridge and the safe deposit area."

So that's why they did a background check on me before I was hired, Millie thought to herself. It made perfect sense.

She swallowed nervously. *It was a good thing the fire department back home had decided not to charge her with arson.*

"I'll guard it with my life," Millie assured them as she slipped it in her front pants pocket.

Donovan glanced around and then motioned Millie and Andy off to one side. "Did you hear what they found shoved in the corner of the closet of Olivia LaShay's cabin?" Donovan whispered.

Andy bent forward, shaking his head.

"An aquarium," Donovan said. "Perfect for keeping a spider."

The muscle in Andy's jaw tightened. "You don't say."

Donovan nodded. "The police are beginning to suspect Olivia's death was a homicide."

Andy turned to Millie. "Pets are strictly prohibited."

Millie's brow arched. She would never consider a venomous spider a pet. Of course, this was Florida and people in Florida were always doing crazy things, at least it seemed that way from watching the news.

If the aquarium wasn't supposed to be on the ship, or in Olivia's room, wouldn't someone have noticed it? Her roommate perhaps? Millie wondered.

Donovan read Millie's mind. "They already questioned Olivia's roommate, Maribelle. She told them that Olivia was deathly afraid of spiders." He shook his head. "On top of that, she'd never seen an aquarium in the cabin before today."

Other staff was beginning to gather behind the desk. "I better get back to work," Donovan said.

Andy and Millie headed towards the stairs. She glanced back at Donovan and his dark head, which was lowered over the notepad again. "He's the purser," she guessed.

"Yes. Donovan is in charge of all the money on the ship. Kind of like a banker," he explained. "We have one more stop to make before you're free to explore the ship on your own."

They walked for several long moments in silence. Millie quickly figured out they were walking toward the front of the ship.

The long hallway abruptly ended and a large, vault-like door covered the wall in front of them. Above the knob was a numbered keypad, along with a slot for key card access.

Andy fished a card from his front shirt pocket and swiped his card through the slot. A high-pitched beep sounded. Andy pushed the door open and stepped inside.

It didn't take but a second to figure out where they were. They were on the bridge. Millie's heart began to pound a bit faster. She had a sneaking suspicion she was about to meet the big shot, the man in charge of it all, the captain of the ship.

Millie swallowed hard as the captain came toward them. At least she thought it was the captain. He looked familiar...

Her eyes widened when she realized it was the man she had bumped into down in the atrium, right after she stumbled upon the young woman's body. He was still wearing the white uniform.

She noticed the bars or stitching on the shoulders of his shirt. Millie assumed that showed his rank as an officer. Captain Stubing from the Love Boat came to mind.

He was tall and muscular, something she hadn't noticed on their last run in. His hair was mostly gray with streaks of black. He gazed down at her and smiled. Somehow, the smile didn't quite reach his eyes.

Millie instantly interpreted the look as a look of disapproval, or maybe he was just having a bad day. She hoped it was the latter.

The introduction was brief and moments later, they stepped back off the bridge and into the hallway. The door closed and Millie turned to Andy. "Is he always that - uh - friendly?" she asked.

Andy shook his head. "Captain Armati can come across as a bit standoffish, but he's not. He just runs a tight ship." Andy chuckled at his own pun. "Tight ship. Get it?"

Millie smiled. Well, at least it wasn't personal...she hoped.

Andy led her back to the atrium. "You're on your own for the rest of the afternoon." He looked down at his watch, and then over at the watch on Millie's wrist. "Good. You have a watch. You'll need it."

"We have a staff show at 8:00 p.m. tonight. The show is kind of a warm up before the passengers arrive tomorrow. Meet me behind the curtains at seven sharp." He didn't wait for a reply before he turned on his heel and walked away.

Millie watched until he disappeared around the corner. She looked at her watch. It was only three o'clock. There was still time to explore the ship.

She glanced around. To her right was the casino. To her left, a row of shops. *I wonder if one of these was where the poor girl had worked.*

She wandered down the hall and glanced inside the first window. Brightly wrapped candies and bags of pink and blue cotton candy filled the shelves. Next to that was a liquor store. In the window was an enormous glass bottle of booze.

When she got to the third store, she noticed the door was open a crack, and could hear the faint strain of music as it wafted through the narrow opening.

Millie's eyes wandered to the glass window and an array of trinkets on display. There were stuffed animals with the ship's logo, coffee mugs and boxes of saltwater taffy. Above that was a collection of T-shirts.

She gently pushed on the open door and peeked inside. The music grew louder. There was another noise. She could hear banging coming from the far corner, behind the checkout counter.

Before she could change her mind, Millie marched inside.

Off to one side was a small glass checkout counter. On top of the counter was a cash register. A mound of grayish black bobbed up and down. It was the top of someone's head.

The beehive bounced around as the person pulled small boxes from a much larger one and set them in neat stacks on a cart nearby.

The only thing in Millie's line of vision was the tip top of the "do," and blood red fingernails.

The massive cone of hair tipped back - just far enough to bump into a glass figurine on the shelf behind her. It teetered for a few brief seconds before falling off the shelf and landing with a muffled thump as it hit the carpeted floor. The woman with the "do" reached forward and picked it up.

Her back was still to Millie as she placed the figurine back on the shelf. Finally, she spun around. Bright green eyes met Millie's eyes.

She stepped out from behind the counter. The woman's form-fitting blazer clung to her hips. She had what Millie quickly decided was an hourglass figure. Raquel Welch came to mind.

Millie frowned and glanced down at her own drab uniform. The woman made her feel old and frumpy, although now that she got a good look, she was probably close to Millie's age.

"I-I'm sorry," Millie stuttered. "I didn't mean to sneak up on you."

The woman's lips curved in a welcoming smile. "Y'all didn't scare me." She reached a hand behind her head and patted the beehive. "This crazy hair is always messin' me up. I'm Catherine, but you can call me Cat."

"I'm Mildred Sanders, the new assistant cruise director," she said. "Uh - You can call me Millie."

"Okay Millie." Cat picked up a small box of key chains. She grabbed a handful of the ship-shaped metal trinkets and began unloading them into a display tray on the edge of the counter. "Are you finding your way around?"

Millie nodded. "Andy gave me a tour and introduced me to a few people, but now I'm striking out on my own."

Cat nodded. "Well, it's nice to meet you." She pulled another box from the cart and set it in front of her. "I was *so* glad to see what's-his-name gone." She shuddered dramatically.

Millie remembered Annette, the head of the food department, had made a similar remark. "I've heard that before. What was so bad about...?"

"Toby," Cat finished. "Or as I liked to call him, 'toady.'" Cat tugged on the bottom of her skirt and stepped out from behind the counter.

Millie glanced down at Cat's shoes. She was wearing leopard print stiletto heels. If Millie had to guess, they were at least six inches high.

Millie would never buy shoes with a heel that high. She would break her neck trying to walk in them, although they would make a perfect weapon if you wanted to...say, for example, strike ones cheating ex-husband in the forehead.

Her eyes traveled back up. The pattern on the shoes matched the leopard print scarf tied around Cat's neck.

Cat walked over to the display case and began rearranging the shelf. "He was a humdinger, that one. A real creep." She shook her head, as if to erase the image of Toby from her mind.

The woman inspected a box of candy before she dropped her hands to her side and her shoulders drooped forward. "Today hasn't been the best of days." Cat grabbed a wayward strand of hair and expertly tucked it back into the beehive. "Did you hear about the girl that died?"

Millie nodded. "I saw her lying on the floor by the bar, right before they covered her body."

Cat nodded. "That was Olivia. She worked here, in the gift shop."

Millie perked up. She'd hoped to find out a little more about the young woman, particularly now that there was a bit of a mystery surrounding her death. "Did you hear how she died?"

Cat nodded. "One of the bartenders, Bobby, was in here a little while ago. Something about a wound on her ankle. He said he heard that it was a spider bite."

Satisfied with her new window display, Cat faced Millie. "That poor girl was deathly afraid of spiders. How ironic is it that she may have died from a venomous bite?"

Millie shook her head. She wasn't sure about the "ironic" part. Her detective radar was in full gear now. The clues were adding up - and it wasn't pointing to a cut and dried "I happened upon a spider" by accident death.

"I don't think it was an accident," Cat said. She opened her mouth and quickly closed it. Millie waited for more, but that was all that Cat had to say, other than, "I better get back to work."

Millie took that as her cue. She waved goodbye and headed out the door. The woman knew something and Millie wished more than anything that she knew what that "something" was.

Chapter 4

Millie wandered out of the gift shop and over to another set of doors on the other side of the corridor. She grinned when she realized the doors were in the shape of a piano. *Ivory Lounge.* It was the piano bar. The door was open and Millie could hear muffled sobs coming from within. She stood to one side, tilted her head, and peeked around the corner.

"You're new."

A male voice with a heavy accent was close to her ear. Too close. Millie whirled around and came face-to-face with a man who was standing in what most people would consider their "personal space."

Millie took a quick step back. The first thing she noticed was that he wasn't wearing a ship's uniform.

"Yes. I'm the new assistant cruise director. My name is Mildred Sanders but you can call me Millie." She groaned inwardly, not sure why she had added that last part, considering she wasn't sure she wanted him calling her Millie.

"Ahh...I see." He returned her small nod with one of his own. "I am Jose Juan Carlos Garcia Santiago Hernandez but you can call me Gary." He gave a small bow.

"Gary." She blinked rapidly. He didn't look like a Gary.

"You like a tour of the ship?"

Millie shook her head. "Andy has already taken care of that. Thank you," she added. The man - Gary - was giving her weird vibes. A chill ran up her spine. There was something about him.

"You w..."

Gary cut her off. "Nice to meet you, Millie." Her name rolled off his tongue, extending the "e" sound and pronouncing it more like Milleeeeeee. He reached for her hand, lifted it to his lips and softly kissed the top.

Millie's mouth dropped open. Before she could reply, he was gone. Right then and there, she decided he was the oddest man she had ever met, at least so far. The day was still young.

Not wanting to chance another encounter with "Gary," Millie headed in the opposite direction.

She walked past the bank of elevators and over to the stairs. There was still a whole lot of ship to cover. Her plan of attack was to start at the top and work her way down.

Out on deck, the crew was hard at work polishing the handrails. In the buffet area, others were running back and forth, arranging tables and setting up stations.

She smiled at the workers, but didn't stop as she continued past the dining room and to a bar in the back. The bar area was like a ghost town.

Millie headed to a set of stairs leading to another, smaller deck area. Off to one side were sliding glass doors. She trudged up a ramp and stepped inside. The air was cool - the space quiet, unlike the area she had just passed through.

According to the ship's map, Millie knew there was a small church sanctuary tucked away in the corner of the ship, close to the top. A small, painted sign hung on the wall nearby, *Sky Chapel*. She was in the right place.

Millie stepped inside the cozy space. The interior was painted white, which made it look a bit bigger than it was. There were two rows of pews and a small aisle separated the pews.

In the front was a stained glass wall. Hanging on the wall was a cross. On both sides of the cross were two artificial windows. In front of that was a small podium.

"Can I help you?"

Millie whirled around. "I-I was just checking out the ship." A gray-haired, middle-aged man stood in the doorway. "Are you the pastor?"

He didn't look like a man of the cloth, dressed in casual shorts and a button down shirt. He looked more like a guest, although that was impossible since there were no guests coming on board the ship until the following day. He nodded. "Pastor Pete Evans, at your service." He smiled and gave a small bend of his waist.

Millie took a step closer. "Do you have regular church services?" She had read on the ship's website that they did.

He nodded. "Yes. The services are nondenominational and are held every Sunday morning at nine a.m."

Millie let out a sigh of relief. She had been involved in her church back home and mostly teaching Sunday school classes or filling in for the choir. It gave her comfort knowing she would at least be able to spend some time in the House of the Lord once a week.

"Care to join me?" He pointed to a nearby pew. Millie slid onto the seat.

He joined her, sitting a short distance away. "You're new on the ship." It wasn't a question.

"Yes. I'm the new assistant cruise director," she told him. "My name is Mildred Sanders, but you can call me Millie."

"Ahh." He nodded. "You'll like Andy," he predicted.

"I already do."

"We've had a bit of excitement today." He crossed his arms and leaned back. "Her name was

Olivia LaShay and she was one of the crew, but I'm sure you've already heard."

Millie nodded.

"She was troubled, it seems."

Millie wondered what he meant by "troubled." She remembered hearing that Olivia had numerous boyfriends. She probably made quite a few enemies. Could it be she'd made an enemy who was angry enough to kill her?

Pastor Evans must have decided he had said too much. He abruptly got to his feet. "I hope to see you Sunday morning, Millie."

"I wouldn't miss it for the world."

Millie wandered out of the sanctuary and down the small ramp, a smile on her face. *The chapel would be her perfect church away from home*, she decided.

It took her another hour to visit every floor and check out the guest areas. Her feet were beginning to ache, so she headed back down to the crew quarters. In her room, she flopped down on the bunk and kicked off her shoes.

The sound of a toilet flushing made her bolt upright. She felt guilty for settling in and immediately hopped off the bed.

Sarah emerged from the bathroom and plopped down in the chair. "How'd it go?"

Millie smiled. "So far, so good. I think I'm going to like it." She looked around the cramped space and jerked her head toward the door. "I have a feeling I'll be spending most of my time out there."

"Yeah, me too. Did you hear anything else about that poor woman who died?"

Millie lifted her hands high above her head and stretched her back. "They think it was a spider bite.

Her roommate found an aquarium in their cabin this morning."

Sarah wandered over to the closet to study her reflection in front of the full-length mirror and adjusted the tag on her shirt. "I heard the same rumor. I met her roommate, Maribelle. She works in the dining room, too. She's really shook up about the whole thing."

"Oh?" Sarah had Millie's undivided attention. "Where's her cabin?"

"It's three doors down and to the right."

Millie made a mental note to remember that as she glanced at her watch. It was time to meet Andy.

Chapter 5

Sarah headed to the crew area while Millie went in the opposite direction down the I-95 corridor. She stopped in front of the metal door she had taken earlier, grateful that she was already starting to learn her way around the ship.

To the left was a bank of elevators. To the right, the stairs. Millie opted for the stairs since she wasn't a huge fan of elevators, not since the time she was in the elevator of the Sears Tower in Chicago, years ago and the elevator decided to stop halfway up.

It was then Millie discovered she suffered from claustrophobia, so elevators were out. Unless it was life or death.

Luckily, the crew areas were on deck one and the theater / stage was on deck three. She stepped inside the theater and headed to the front. She heard Andy and his big, booming voice before she saw him. He was off to one side, talking to one of the young male dancers, his face buried in his hands.

Andy placed a hand on his shoulder. "You can do this, Zack. You have to. You're a performer - a professional. The show must go on."

"But I can't. Her face...it's there every time I close my eyes." Anguished cries rocked his body.

Millie slid a chair close to the young man and sat down on the edge of the seat. She had no idea what was going on, but she had a sneaking suspicion it had something to do with Olivia - the dead girl.

She touched his arm. "Is there anything I can do?"

The young man, Zack, lifted his head. Hollow, grief-filled eyes stared into Millie's eyes. "Can you bring Olivia back?"

Andy took this as his cue to leave and made a hasty exit. She watched him retreat and then turned her attention to the heartbroken young man.

"We can pray for her and her family." *And pray that God would comfort this poor man*, Millie silently added.

They lowered their heads and Millie offered a small prayer for the girl she had never met. "Lord, we pray for peace and comfort for Zack, for Olivia and for Olivia's family. We pray that Olivia is now safely in Your arms."

Zack lifted his head and wiped his eyes. "Thanks." He glanced at her tag. "Thanks, Millie. That helped a lot."

The dancers began filing out of the dressing area and onto the stage. It was show time.

Millie stood next to Andy as the two of them watched the show from the sideline. It gave her a completely different perspective from that angle.

She was able to chat with a few of the performers before they went on, and they were a bunch of characters.

She decided they were probably a whole lot of fun to hang out with - if she were at least thirty years younger.

After the show ended, the performers changed out of their costumes and into crew outfits. Andy grabbed a clipboard that was hanging on the wall and began to make his way down the checklist as he meticulously counted the costumes and headpieces.

"Tomorrow I'll teach you how to inventory the costumes." He glanced around and lowered his voice. "You would be amazed at how many of these expensive pieces somehow manage to sprout legs and wander off, never to be seen again."

After Andy finished, he locked the dressing room door and the two of them made their way off the stage. The theater was empty. Millie shivered, as she looked up at the cavernous ceiling, relieved she wasn't alone.

They parted ways just outside the theater with Andy mumbling something about getting a jump-start on tomorrow's schedule.

Not certain what else she should do, Millie headed down to the crew dining room. It had been hours since she'd eaten and her stomach began to grumble. The smell of fried foods and sizzling burgers filled the cafeteria.

There were only a handful of employees inside. She grabbed a tray at the end of the line and moved forward. She eyed the burgers sizzling on the grill and could feel her arteries hardening.

Millie sighed and reached for a salad before moving on.

A young woman, her hair pulled back in a long, dark ponytail, came up beside her. Millie glanced at her tag, *Maribelle*.

She wondered if this was Olivia's cabin mate. She didn't have to wonder long. A man on the other side approached the counter. "How are you holding up, Maribelle?"

"Not good, Josh. They're saying Olivia was murdered." Tears welled up in the young woman's eyes.

Josh raised his brows. "Murdered?"

"Olivia was bitten by a spider and it wasn't an accident." She lowered her voice, but not enough so that Millie couldn't hear. "They're questioning me, as if I had something to do with her death."

Millie reluctantly moved on. It would look suspicious if she continued to stand in the same spot. She edged forward and reached for an apple.

Maribelle and Josh followed her down the line. The man behind the line rearranged the array of desserts. "How do they know it was a spider? Did they find it?"

Maribelle shuddered. "Nope and they won't switch my room. I won't be able to sleep tonight, wondering if something is crawling on me." She rubbed her arms, as if to brush off an invisible spider.

Millie reached the end of the line and Josh had moved on. "I heard about that poor girl," she said. "Do they really think someone murdered her?"

Maribelle grabbed a turkey and Swiss cheese sandwich and followed Millie toward the tables. "*I* think someone killed her," she confessed. "They found an aquarium buried in the bottom of Olivia's closet, but it did not belong to Olivia, I can promise you that."

Millie wandered over to the nearest empty table and sat down. She held her breath, hoping Maribelle would join her.

The girl slid into the seat across from her.

"Do you have any idea who would have motive to kill her? I heard they thought maybe she'd been bitten before she got back on the ship." Of course, that was before they found the spider's home inside the cabin.

She didn't wait for Maribelle to answer. "Why do you think you're a suspect?" Millie asked.

Maribelle tore the crust from her sandwich and dropped it on the edge of the plate. "Olivia and I had a bit of a falling out just before her death," she confessed. "A very public falling out. I told her I wished she was dead and a bunch of people heard me."

Millie tore the packet of ranch dressing open and dumped it on her salad. She popped a forkful of lettuce along with a cucumber into her mouth and chewed thoughtfully. "I heard that Olivia had quite a few enemies on the ship."

"That was because she made it her personal goal to steal everyone's boyfriend, including mine."

Maribelle's statement certainly gave her motive. Of course, it gave a lot of others on board motive, as well. Still, she would be the most likely suspect and the one who was closest to her. Motive and opportunity.

"Who do you think killed Olivia?" Millie asked.

"I think it was Cat," Maribelle whispered.

Cat...Cat... "You mean the lady who runs the gift shop?"

"Olivia was spreading rumors, telling everyone Cat was about to be fired and that she was going to get her job," Maribelle lifted what was left of the top piece of bread from her sandwich, pulled out a wilting piece of lettuce and tossed it on the plate next to the discarded bread. "Olivia was a compulsive liar so, whether or not that was true?" The young woman shrugged.

80

Millie tapped the tines of her fork on the edge of her plate. That was motive. "Anyone else you think might be a prime suspect?"

Maribelle was turning out to be a wealth of information. "There's one more. At least, one more that *I* think could be capable of murder."

Millie held her breath, waiting for Maribelle to go on.

"Andy."

"Andy?" Millie's eyes widened. "Do you mean Andy, the Cruise Director, Andy?"

Maribelle nodded. "He always kind of had a thing for Olivia. Of course, they all did. She started getting these odd little notes and for some reason, she was convinced they were coming from him. Whenever I questioned her about it, she would clam up."

Millie remembered Andy being on the scene when they covered the body. *Was she working for a killer?*

"Do you know if the notes are still around?"

Maribelle dabbed at the corner of her mouth and threw her napkin on top of the uneaten food. "Yeah. She hid them in our cabin. I completely forgot about them until just now when you reminded me."

Millie sprang to her feet. Her belt caught the edge of the tray and almost flipped it over. She grabbed the tray to stop the contents from hitting the floor. "Can I see them?"

"My shift on deck starts in fifteen minutes. I can take you down to my room now if you want."

"If you don't mind." Millie scooped up her trash, dumped it on the tray and darted over to the trash bin before Maribelle could change her mind.

She followed the woman out of the cafeteria and down the hall. Sarah was right. Maribelle's room was only a few doors down from theirs.

Maribelle slipped her card in the slot and pushed the door open. Millie followed her in.

The room was identical to Millie's, except a whole lot messier. "Are you getting a new cabin mate?' Millie asked.

Maribelle strode over to the bunks, lifted the mattress on the upper bunk and stuck her hand underneath. "I haven't heard yet." She pulled out a small pile of papers. There were three sheets of paper in all. She handed them to Millie.

On the cover of the top note was a sketch of a cruise ship. In the far, right-hand corner were the words *Siren of the Seas*.

Millie held the sheet close to her face and squinted at the words. Luckily, she'd remembered to bring her reading glasses with her. She slipped them on and the words came into focus.

She read the first note aloud:

"You are so beautiful, Olivia. I long for the day I can tell you face-to-face how much I love you."

She folded the paper and slipped it under the other two. She read the second one:

"I caught you talking to Darna the other night and it made me angry. Why are you trying to make me jealous?"

Millie looked up at Maribelle. "Who is Darna?"

"Darna is a bartender. He spends most of his time working down at the atrium bar," Maribelle answered. The atrium bar. It was the same bar where Olivia had died.

Millie read the third note:

"Zack is not the one for you, Olivia. He doesn't love you like I do. If you don't stop seeing him, I'll be forced to stop you."

That sounded like a threat to Millie. It also sounded like a real psycho. This was not going to be an easy case to solve. Olivia had more enemies than Bonnie and Clyde.

Millie handed the notes back to Maribelle. "What about Zack? Do you think he's capable of murder?"

Maribelle's expression crumpled. It dawned on Millie that Zack had been Maribelle's boyfriend and Olivia had stolen him from her. She reached out and touched the woman's hand. "I'm sorry. I had no idea."

"It's okay." Maribelle sniffled and wiped her eyes. "I mean, if he really loved me, he wouldn't just up and leave me at the crook of Olivia's finger."

She had a point. No man was worth it if he left her for another woman. *Like Roger.*

Poor Maribelle. She had lost her boyfriend. It looked as if someone had murdered her roommate and she was a suspect. On top of that, there was a good chance she had a deadly spider roaming around her cabin.

"Thank you for showing those notes to me. You really should turn those over to authorities."

Maribelle nodded. "I'll take care of it tomorrow." Her eyes narrowed as a sudden thought occurred to her. Millie worked for Andy. *Had Andy set Millie up to question her, to try to find out what Olivia might have said to her?*

Maribelle's mouth drew into a thin, straight line. "I should get upstairs," she said stiffly.

She didn't wait for Millie to reply as she walked to the door and opened it. She waited for Millie to step out before she closed the door and abruptly marched off.

Something had changed Maribelle's attitude and Millie was at a loss. She watched the woman walk down the long corridor and then disappear out of sight.

Millie headed back to her own cabin. She pulled out the small chair and plopped down before grabbing a pad of paper and pencil from the desk drawer.

At the top of the small sheet of paper, she wrote the word *Suspect* and underlined it. The first name she put on the list was Maribelle.

Under Maribelle, she wrote Andy's name, although she didn't want to. She added Zack and Darna to the list.

Last, but not least, she wrote Cat's name. Five suspects. Five people she needed to check out.

Satisfied she'd had a good first day on the job and that her investigation was shaping up nicely, Millie changed into her pajamas and brushed her teeth. She crawled into bed and shut off the light.

Millie closed her eyes and began to pray. "Thank you, Lord, for giving me a good first day and for all the other blessings in my life. For the first time in a long time, I wasn't alone or lonely. Please help me to do the best job ever and if You don't mind, please help me solve Olivia LaShay's murder. Thank You for Your Son, my Savior, Jesus Christ."

Millie wasn't scheduled to work until noon the next day, which meant she would have time to attend the church service upstairs before guests started arriving. The thought was no more out of her head, when she closed her eyes and promptly fell asleep. She didn't even hear Sarah come into the cabin hours later.

Chapter 6

Ding...ding... Millie pried one eye open. For a moment, she couldn't remember where she was or where the strange noise was coming from. Then it dawned on her. It was the alarm on her wristwatch.

Millie groped above her head as she reached for the light switch when she remembered Sarah. She could hear the faint sound of snoring.

She quietly flung the covers back and tiptoed to the bathroom. She'd placed her church clothes - one of the skirts she'd brought with her, and a pink button-down blouse, in the bathroom before she went to bed so she could get ready without disturbing Sarah.

When she stepped out of the bathroom half an hour later, Sarah was awake and the TV set was on. "I'm sorry. I didn't mean to wake you."

Sarah smiled. "You didn't. I woke up on my own." She stretched her arms as far above her head as the ceiling would allow. "I have an internal alarm clock," she joked. "It goes off every morning at 7:30 a.m."

She eyed Millie's skirt and shirt. "You're all dressed up."

"I'm heading to the chapel for the Sunday service."

Sarah nodded. "Maybe next week I'll go with you," she told her as she swung her legs over the side of the bunk and dropped to the floor.

Millie glanced at her watch. If she didn't get a move on, she would be late for church.

When she stepped inside the chapel, she was surprised to discover that it was almost full. Of course, full was only around forty people.

Several seated guests eyed her curiously. One of them was Annette, the food director. She scooched over and waved to Millie.

Millie slid onto the hard, wooden bench. "Thanks for the seat," she said gratefully.

"The more, the merrier. I come every Sunday, when my schedule allows. Most of us here are regulars."

Millie recognized a few others she had seen around the ship.

"How did you fare your first day on the job?" Annette seemed genuinely interested.

"The job is great." She changed the subject. "Did you happen to know Olivia, the young woman who died?"

"I only knew her by name. She had quite a reputation on the ship." Annette started to say something else and then stopped. "I don't want to be one to gossip. Let's just say, she had her share of enemies."

Annette straightened her back. "Hey. I heard someone and I think it was Andy, tell me you and your husband used to own a detective agency."

Millie's face warmed at the thought of her cheating husband. "Yeah. He did the detective work while I worked behind the scenes. You know, paperwork, billing. The boring stuff. I was always interested in the sleuthing end of it. Sometimes I even helped Roger, my ex-husband, out in the field."

Annette raised her eyebrows. "So are you doing a little detective work on this one?"

Millie wasn't sure if she would get in trouble for poking around. "I have to say that I'm curious to find out how that young woman died."

Annette made a confession of her own. "I just love a good mystery. My favorite show is 'Murder, We Wrote.'"

Millie didn't have a chance to reply. Pastor Evans stepped to the podium. The congregation stood and they sang a few hymns from the hymnbooks that were under the pews. After the singing ended, Pastor Evans talked about having faith and hope in the Lord. The key scripture was:

"For I know the plans I have for you," declares the Lord, "plans to prosper you and not harm you, plans to give you hope and a future." Jeremiah 29:11 NIV

The message had Millie's name written all over it.

When the service ended, Annette and Millie wandered out of the small sanctuary and onto the back deck. "Do you have any suspects yet?" Annette asked.

Millie grinned. "Yep. I guess I do."

"Let me guess." She didn't give Millie a chance to reply. "One of them has to be Cat."

"Yep."

Annette tapped the top of the railing with her nail. "Then I would add Olivia's roommate - what is her name? Clarabelle? Annabelle?"

"Maribelle," Millie answered.

"I have a suspect of my own," Annette added mysteriously.

Millie was all ears. "Who?"

Annette glanced around. "Doctor Gundervan. I caught him arguing with Olivia the day before she died."

Millie shook her head. The girl sure did make her rounds - and enemies.

"You know, I did get a bit of a grease burn earlier. I should have Doctor Gundervan take a look at it." Annette winked. "What if *you* go with me to visit the doctor? We could kill two birds with one stone, so to speak. I get to see how you interrogate...uh...question a suspect and you get to meet the doctor."

Millie glanced at her watch. If the doctor was around, she would have just enough time to meet him before heading back to the cabin to change into her work clothes and report to work. "It might work if we hurry."

Millie followed Annette down the stairs. She had never noticed a doctor's office on board the ship and it didn't take long for her to figure out why. It was down on deck two, near the passenger exit and right next to a door marked *Security*.

Annette eased the door marked *Medical Center,* open. Inside the room was a cozy sitting area. A blood pressure cuff and small table with a row of glass jars sat in the corner. Beyond that was another open door.

Millie could see two hospital beds pushed up against a stark, white wall. A tall, red cabinet separated the beds.

She started to walk through the second door when a young man wearing a white button down shirt appeared. Around his neck was a stethoscope. "Hello, Annette."

He was young. Much younger than Millie had envisioned and she immediately wondered if Olivia had been having a fling with the doctor. She glanced at his finger, and spotted what appeared to be a wedding band.

"Hi, Doctor Gundervan." Annette held out her right hand. "I burned my hand this morning on one of those Sterno cans and was wondering if you could take a quick peek at it."

He inspected Annette's microscopic wound while Annette jerked her head at Millie.

Millie frowned. She had never actually interrogated anyone before. That had always been Roger's job.

"This doesn't look too bad." He grabbed a tube from one of the drawers inside the red cabinet and glanced at Millie's tag as he unscrewed the top. "Millie." He smiled. "So you're the new assistant cruise director."

"Yeah. I thought I would run down here with Annette so I could meet you. Not that I hope I ever have to see you again," she joked. *Smooth. Real smooth*, she berated herself.

Annette was giving her that look, as if to say, *"Aren't you going to ask him anything?"*

Millie laughed nervously. "Yeah, yesterday was a little stressful. The first thing I came across as soon as I got on the ship was a woman lying on the floor in the atrium."

Doctor Gundervan's head shot up. "Such a shame and a waste of a young life."

He turned his attention back to Annette's injured hand as he dabbed ointment on it. "They brought her down here before the ambulance arrived. It looked as if she may have been bitten by an envielous spider, a nocturnal and poisonous spider."

"I ran into the woman's roommate, Maribelle," Millie said. "She told me Olivia had plenty of enemies and that the authorities didn't think her death was an accident."

Doctor Gundervan screwed the top back on the tube and dropped it in the drawer. "I wouldn't know anything about that." He stepped over to the small sink. "I think I met her maybe once in passing."

He turned to Annette as he grabbed a paper towel to dry his hands. "Did you need anything else?"

"No. I think I'm all set. Thanks, doc. It feels better already."

The women made their way out of the center, back into the hall and out of earshot. "Did you hear that? He said he never knew her," Annette whispered.

Millie nodded. How could Doctor Gundervan have a heated argument with someone he claims he didn't know?

Chapter 7

Millie met Andy near the passenger entrance, their prearranged meeting place, for what Andy jokingly referred to as "show time." She smiled as she watched the passengers walk through the door and catch their first glimpse of the magnificent cruise ship.

"Welcome aboard." Andy's booming voice echoed over and over. He was in his element. It was obvious Andy loved his job. She glanced at him out of the corner of her eye. He didn't *look* like a killer...

Millie quickly figured out which passengers were the newbies and which ones had cruised before. Her favorites were the ones who had never been on a cruise ship. The expressions on their faces were priceless as they stared in awe at the size and elegance of the ship.

A handful of passengers wandered over to Andy and Millie. Some of them had questions, but others recognized him. Millie was amazed when he even greeted some of them by name.

There were thousands of passengers sailing this voyage and each week the names and faces changed. How he could remember even one of them astonished her.

After the last passenger had boarded, the doors closed and the long, glass ramp pulled away from the ship. Millie swallowed hard. This was it. This was her home and this was her job. Fortunately, she didn't have time to dwell on it.

Andy leaned to the side and lowered his voice. "I trust you had a nice morning off."

Millie nodded. "I went to church."

"Annette Delacroix attends the service." He headed for the office and Millie followed behind.

"Today is a full day for us. Bingo starts in ten minutes. After that, there's a trivia contest in the Paradise Lounge. Starting at two o'clock is the belly flop competition out on the lido deck, followed by the art auction at three o'clock, which coincides with wine tasting in the atrium."

He waited for Millie to catch up. "There's no need to worry about the art auction. That's run by a separate company."

Millie nodded. She didn't know that but filed it in the "need to know" section of her brain.

Andy and she headed to the theater to prepare for the evening's first show. The dancers and performers were already practicing behind the red velvet curtains.

Millie made a beeline for Zack. "Are you feeling better today?"

"Yes, ma'am. Thank you so much for your prayers."

The afternoon flew by as Millie and Andy moved from one event to the other. She was so busy, she completely forgot about lunch. When six o'clock rolled around and it was time for her hour break, she was starving.

Andy had told her she could eat in Waves, the buffet area, and mingle with the guests. In fact, he had encouraged her, so that guests would feel comfortable approaching her with questions and comments.

Millie headed to the least busy buffet line, the salad bar, and grabbed a plate. Sarah came up behind her, rag in hand. "How's it going?" she asked.

"So far, so good." Millie strategically arranged several tomatoes on top of her mound of lettuce. "How about you?"

"Same here. Very busy, but fun." Sarah looked around before she lowered her head and whispered,

"Nikki told me Maribelle, Olivia LaShay's roommate, is a suspect in her murder."

Millie paused in front of the dressings. *Ranch or blue cheese?* She grabbed the container of ranch dressing. "I talked to Maribelle earlier. It seems that a lot of people had reason to want Olivia out of the picture, not just Maribelle." She didn't mention the notes that Maribelle had shown her.

Sarah shivered. "At least I'm not on the list of suspects."

Millie watched Sarah walk away. *That was kind of an odd comment,* Millie decided. *Why would she be a suspect? She wasn't even an employee when it happened.*

She shrugged it off and turned to face the seating area. Millie smiled at several of the families as she slid into a nearby booth. It made her a little sad as she thought about her own family.

Millie reminded herself that *she* made this decision, that this was something *she* wanted to try. Plus, the contract was only for eight months. After the eight months, she could decide if she wanted to stay on or go home, if they even wanted her.

She ate her salad in record time and turned her attention to the hot food section. Her stomach was still grumbling. Millie had passed trays of pasta on the way to the salad bar and it looked tempting. Since this was her only meal of the day, she decided to fix a plate before heading back to work.

Millie filled her plate with a heaping spoonful of macaroni and cheese. Next, she added a large slice of lasagna.

She grabbed a piece of garlic bread before heading to the carving station. Her mouth watered at the sight of the roasted turkey. The man behind the Plexiglas smiled as he laid a thick slice of meat on top of her mound of macaroni.

When she got back to her table, she realized she had forgotten to pray. Her routine was so different now. Millie bowed her head and prayed over her food. When she lifted her head, she caught a glimpse of Zack, the dancer. He was standing in front of the salad bar and noticed her at the exact same moment. He finished fixing his plate and made his way over to the table. "Do you mind if I join you?"

"No, please do." Millie moved the half-eaten bite of turkey to the side of her cheek. "Have a seat."

Zack slid in and scoped out her plate of food. "Your pasta looks delicious."

"It is." Millie lifted her napkin from her lap and dabbed at the corners of her mouth. "You should try it."

Zack shook his head and patted his stomach. "No can do. It would ruin my girlish - or should I say - boyish figure."

Millie grinned. She was thankful that the least of her concerns was how much pasta she was eating. "How are you doing, Zack?"

"I...I'm okay." Zack unfolded the napkin, placed it in his lap and picked up his fork. "Today is better than yesterday."

Millie nodded as she tore off a chunk of garlic bread. "I'm glad to hear that."

"I heard they think someone murdered Olivia."

"Yeah and one of the suspects is her roommate, Maribelle," Millie said.

He nodded. "They were best of friends, at least for a while. Maribelle and I dated briefly. Maribelle seemed to think that Olivia stole me from her, but that's not true."

Millie slid the turkey across her plate and sliced a piece. She offered it to Zack. "Would you like to try a bite?"

He started to say no, but then changed his mind as he plucked the piece of meat from the tip of the fork and popped it in his mouth. "That's good."

"Were you dating Maribelle right before Olivia?"

"Yeah," Zack admitted. "But it was nothing serious with Maribelle. Not like it was with Olivia."

Millie frowned. From all that she'd heard about Olivia, she wasn't the type to keep a boyfriend for very long. Olivia must not have had time to grow weary of Zack.

Millie switched gears. "Do you know Doctor Gundervan?"

Zack nodded. "He's been the ship's doctor for a few years now. The first time I met him was a couple of weeks ago when Olivia pulled a muscle in her back and she had to go see him. She was in bad shape."

Millie paused, her fork full of pasta halfway to her mouth. "Doctor Gundervan treated Olivia?"

"Yeah." Zack finished his salad in record time. He threw his napkin on top of the empty plate. "He gave her some pain pills, which seemed to help."

Millie frowned. This meant that the doctor *was* lying and he *had* known Olivia.

"It was kind of funny now that I think about it. When I took her down there that day, she made it seem like they didn't know each other, but when we walked in the door he greeted her by name."

Zack glanced up at the clock on the wall. "I gotta get back to work."

"I'm right behind you." Millie threw her napkin on top of her dirty plate and followed Zack out. They crossed the lido deck, and made their way down the stairs and into the theater. Once again, she made it in the nick of time.

Andy was in the thick of things, barking orders and waving his clipboard in the air like a wild man. He swung around when he heard Zack and Millie's steps echo across the stage floor. "Once again, you made it with a minute to spare."

Millie smiled sheepishly and made a mental note to keep better track of her time - something she wasn't used to doing.

The production show, *Melody of the Seas,* went off without a hitch. Millie had watched the show the night before and thoroughly enjoyed it, but somehow the energy and interaction from the passengers made it even better.

Zack high-fived Millie as he exited the stage. She really liked the young man. He reminded her of her own son, Blake.

She drew in a quick breath. *Hopefully he wasn't the killer.*

The show had taken five costume changes. Andy stood off to the side and watched as two of the backstage assistants sorted through the towering heap of costumes the dancers had dumped in the center of the dressing room floor.

He eyed Millie over the top of his clipboard. "You've taken a liking to Zack."

"He reminds me of my own son."

Andy shifted his feet and studied Millie. "I never married myself. Got started in show business right out of high school and traveled around the world until I joined Majestic Cruise Lines years ago," he told her.

Millie's radar went up. This was the perfect opportunity to ask him about Olivia. "No serious girlfriends?"

Two of the female dancers walked by. Andy waited until they were gone. "There was one. Back home in Gloucestershire." His eyes gave off a distant look. "Victoria Dowden."

Millie repeated the name several times in her head. It helped her remember names. That and word association.

Victoria Dowden = Victoria. Like Millie's own car - a Crown Victoria that was back in Michigan, parked in her garage, and Dowden was like dowry, as in getting married.

"What happened?" Millie held her breath. She hoped she hadn't overstepped her boundaries. She had only known Andy a grand total of about twenty-four hours, give or take a couple hours.

Andy was silent as he watched a worker pick up a long, silky scarf and drape it over the top of one of the outfits. "A few months before our wedding Victoria was crossing the street near her house and was struck by a car. She died on the way to the hospital." He lowered his gaze. "I didn't even get a chance to tell her good-bye."

Millie's heart went out to Andy. What a tragic story. "I'm sorry to hear that." She couldn't imagine loving someone and being close to marrying them and then having them die unexpectedly.

She thought of Roger, her cheating ex. All joking aside, she didn't wish him dead. After all, he had given her two beautiful children.

After each outfit and accessory was back in its proper place, and the workers had finished straightening up the make-up area, Andy and she stepped out of the theater. "There's a late night comedy show in the Paradise Lounge, but there's no need for us to make an appearance."

He went on. "If you can make a run by the Tahitian Nights Dance Club and make sure they don't need anything, you're free for the rest of the evening." He glanced at his watch. "It's ten now.

You can report to my office at 7:30 in the morning. Tomorrow is a port day, so we'll have to be near the gang plank to see guests off."

Millie nodded. That meant she had nine and a half hours to grab a snack, get some rest and last, but not least, meet up with Annette to see if she'd discovered any new clues about the murder.

Chapter 8

Millie heard the Tahitian Nights Dance Club before she saw it. Loud, thumping music vibrated the floor outside the lounge. Bright, neon lights flashed through the glass windows. When the lights flashed, she could see inside and the place was packed.

She pushed the heavy glass door and stepped inside. The room was full of young people out on the dance floor, in the chairs and seated at the bar.

Millie wandered over to the bar area. The young man behind the counter was mixing a drink. She had never met him before.

He handed the drink to the girl at the bar, wiped his hands on a towel and stepped over to Millie. Now that he was closer, she could make out his name, *Robert*. "Hello."

Millie cupped her hands to her mouth and spoke loudly. "I'm Millie, the assistant cruise director. I'm here to see if you need anything."

Robert leaned in; his ear turned toward Millie, and shook his head. "I'm all set."

Two young people popped up on the barstools next to Millie, drink cards in hand. Robert poured two Cokes and slid them across the bar.

Millie waited for them to move away and pointed to the radio on her hip. "If you need anything, I'll have this on for another hour or so."

The music stopped and the noise level dropped off.

Robert grabbed some dirty glasses and set them in the sink. "I heard you were snooping around in Olivia's murder case."

Millie leaned her elbows on the countertop. "Where'd you hear that?"

"This ship is like a small town. You would be surprised at how fast news spreads." He shrugged. "Olivia had plenty of enemies."

It was apparent Robert knew a few of the suspects or knew Olivia personally. Maybe Olivia had caught him in her snare. "Who do you think had the most motive to kill her?"

Robert's eyes met Millie's eyes. *She seemed like a nice enough lady*, he decided. Kind of like a grandmother. He had heard all about the new assistant cruise director, that she was older...and nosy. "The obvious person would be her cabin mate, Maribelle."

He picked up a couple more dirty glasses. "But that's too obvious of a suspect. I think someone is trying to frame Maribelle."

The thought had crossed Millie's mind. If Maribelle had killed Olivia using a poisonous spider, wouldn't she at least have enough common sense to get rid of the evidence? It didn't make sense to have the spider roaming around her cabin.

The DJ was back behind the sound booth and began tuning the amp.

Robert leaned forward. "Your boss, Andy, had a thing for her," he said.

Millie nodded, but didn't answer. Maribelle had told her the exact same thing.

Loud music blared through the speakers. There was no way they could carry on a conversation.

Millie gave a small wave and stepped out of the room. It was time to talk to the bartender in the atrium, Darna.

First, she needed to make a pit stop to freshen up and check her uniform. Public restrooms were everywhere, including one that was right outside the lounge.

Satisfied she was up to snuff, she exited the small bathroom and headed out the door, right past the Tahitian Nights club. She glanced in the door and what she saw made her pause.

There at the bar, talking to Robert, was Maribelle. Their heads were close together and they were deep in conversation. They didn't notice Millie watching them.

Millie slid to the side and peeked around the corner where she had a clear view of the two. Robert cupped his hands to his mouth and said something in Maribelle's ear.

She watched for a few moments as they continued to talk. Maribelle stepped onto the footrest and then leaned over the side as Robert caressed her cheek.

Millie took a step back and turned on her heel as she circled around back, out of view of the lounge area. No wonder Robert wanted to steer Millie away from Maribelle. What she had just witnessed added a new twist to the investigation.

The atrium bar was empty with only a handful of guests occupying the chairs as they listened to the piano player. She made a beeline for the bar area and hopped up onto the stool. Her heart sank when she laid eyes on the bartender.

The young woman smiled at Millie. "Can I get you something?"

"I was hoping Darna was working tonight."

The bartender shook her head. "Darna left about half an hour ago."

Millie started to ask when he would be back, but the girl answered her question without her having to ask. "His shift tomorrow is 8:00 a.m. to 5:00 p.m."

Millie did some quick mental calculations. If she took her break around noon, she could stop back by during Darna's shift. "Thanks."

She slid off the barstool and headed to the kitchen in search of Annette. Her heart sank when she noticed the kitchen was dark. Millie's investigation was at a standstill, at least for tonight.

***

Millie stood beside Andy as they smiled and waved good-bye to passenger after passenger as they descended the gangplank and exited the ship. Today was the first port stop and they were in the Bahamas. Nassau to be exact.

Millie and Roger had visited Nassau shortly before he confessed to his affair with the home wrecker, Delilah. She remembered how excited they had been to arrive on the island. They had spent the day touring the pirate museum and gardens, and then stopped for an authentic Bahamian lunch not far from the port.

Unexpected tears filled her eyes. *Why did Roger have to go and ruin it?* Millie wiped the back of her hand across her eyes, hoping that Andy hadn't noticed.

But he had. His eyes filled with concern and he touched her arm. "Are you okay, Millie?"

The lump in Millie's throat refused to budge. The only thing she could do was nod.

Thankfully, a guest approached just then and asked about the ship's sail time and when they needed to be back on board the ship. By the time Andy finished the conversation, Millie had a grip on her emotions. She shoved them to the back of her mind, just as she always had.

Millie wondered if that was why she had become emotionally involved in the investigation. It was her way of proving to Roger, to her family and friends that she had been worth keeping.

Andy didn't ask her again, but he did give her a couple of sympathetic glances. "Why don't you head upstairs for a bite to eat?"

"I think I will." Millie headed to the lido deck to grab a quick lunch. Trivia would be starting soon. It would be her first time striking out on her own and working alone, which made her somewhat nervous.

She felt a bit better when she discovered the trivia contest was on something she was familiar with: Everything 70's. Millie remembered that era well...bell-bottom pants, disco music, and roller-skating.

She grabbed a hot sandwich from the deli and made her way down to the atrium. It was time to meet Darna at the bar.

She ran into Annette in the stairwell. "I've been looking all over for you." Annette was dressed for work in an all-white jacket and white slacks. She was wearing all white except for a smidgen of something dark on the edge of her left sleeve.

Annette looked down when she noticed Millie staring. "Chocolate," she explained. "We're trying a new recipe for our hot lava cake." She put three fingertips to her lips and made a kissing motion. "It's to die for. Of course, not literally. Which reminds me, I know Andy is a primary suspect, along with Doctor Gundervan and Olivia's roommate, Maribelle, but what about Toby?"

Millie shifted her food plate to the other hand. "Toby...but where's the motive?" She remembered the notes that Maribelle had shown her. Toby, Andy, or even the doctor could've sent the notes to Olivia, but that didn't make any of them a killer.

Annette rubbed her hands together. "What do we do next?"

Other than talk to Darna, Millie didn't really have a "next." After all, this was her first case. Roger had never really shared his step-by-step method for investigating or solving his mysteries. Looking back now, she wished she had asked more questions and paid better attention to the details. *Tied him up and thrown him in the river...*

She shook her head to clear the evil thoughts that were creeping in. "I'm on my way to talk to Darna," she said.

"Darna the bartender?" Annette crossed her arms. "Yeah, that makes sense. He and Olivia were tight, you know. They hung out together on their days off."

That seemed a bit odd to Millie considering Zack was her boyfriend-of-the-month at the time of her death. "What about Zack, the dancer?"

Annette waved her hand dismissively. "Zack was just her little minion. I think she was using him.

Olivia had him at her beck and call. Poor boy. She would say jump and he'd ask how high."

The women reached the atrium, and Annette trailed behind Millie as they made their way over to the bar area. She set her plate of food on top of the bar and hopped onto the barstool. Annette hopped onto the seat beside her.

The bartender had his back to them. He was shaking a stainless steel container back and forth. He turned around and gave the two women a sideways glance as he removed the lid from the container and poured liquid into a martini glass.

He slid the glass to a young woman seated in front of him before swiping her card and setting that, along with the receipt, on top.

Annette cast a suspicious glance as she watched the young woman, dressed in one of the shortest dresses Millie had ever seen, walk away. "I hope he carded her."

Millie was thinking the same thing. Of course, the older she got, the younger these women looked...like middle schoolers. She picked up her pickle spear and bit the end as she studied Darna, who didn't look like a "Darna" at all, although she had never known anyone named Darna, so maybe that had something to do with it.

She pictured a dark, mysterious man. The man behind the counter had short blonde hair and it was smoothed back.

He was tall and thin as a rail, with just a hint of a moustache on his upper lip. Millie had read the employee handbook. She knew facial hair was a "no-no" for crew, although staff was a different story, which was how Andy got away with it. Somehow, the look worked for Darna and somehow, she had a feeling that Darna did as he darn well pleased.

Millie and Annette were the only ones at the bar now. He made his way over to the other end. "Two of the most beautiful women on board have come to pay me a visit," he flirted. "To what do I owe this honor?"

Millie immediately liked him. His face was kind and warm, his smile genuine. Annette snatched a fry from Millie's plate. "Millie is here to meet the famous Darna."

He put one hand across his stomach and the other behind his back before he took a bow. "At your service." The smile vanished as he leaned on the counter and cupped his chin in his hand.

Annette didn't wait for Millie to start the interrogation, uh, investigation. "We're here to ask you about Olivia."

"Cat told me they're treating her death as a homicide."

Millie nodded. "I heard you and Olivia were good friends and I was hoping you could tell me a little bit about her." She took a bite of her sandwich.

"Olivia and I were close. We almost always spent our free days together hanging out."

"How long have you known Olivia?" Annette asked.

Darna opened his mouth and then closed it. Millie could see he wasn't sure if he should answer the question.

"Yeah, can I get some service down here?" A man at the other end was waving his card in their direction.

"Be right back." Darna headed to the other end of the bar to take the man's order.

"He's hiding something," Annette whispered in a low voice.

Millie nodded. "Yes. I believe you're right."

They waited for Darna to return. "Can I get you ladies a Coke or water or something?"

"I'll take a water." Millie glanced at her wristwatch. Trivia started in ten minutes. She took a huge bite of sandwich and chewed as fast as her jaws would allow.

Darna set the water in front of her and watched her chew. "Looks like you're gonna need this."

Annette grabbed a second fry from Millie's plate and pointed it at Darna. "You were about to tell us how long you'd known Olivia."

Darna ran a hand over the top of his jelled locks. He lowered his voice and leaned in. "I've known Olivia my whole life," he said. "She was my sister."

Chapter 9

Millie nearly fell off the barstool...*Darna and Olivia were brother and sister?* Millie had read the company handbook from front to back. She knew that it was against company policy for family to work on the same ship, and that included brother and sister.

"We kept it a secret." Darna's jaw tightened. "It was against company policy and if anyone found out, we both would have been fired."

Annette smacked the top of the counter. "Holy smokes. I had no idea."

Darna's eyes filled with tears. "I couldn't even go home to tell my parents about Olivia. The company sent a representative."

Millie's heart went out to Darna. Poor thing. His sister had died right before his eyes. He couldn't even properly mourn her death. She reached out and squeezed his hand. "I am so sorry Darna, but why not admit it now?"

He shook his head. "They would still fire me," he answered. "I need this job. My family relies on my income to survive. I have a young son back home to support."

Millie knew all about how the crew came from countries with little resources and how the workers would take every penny they earned and send it back home.

Right then and there, she vowed to add Darna and all of the other crew to her prayer list. It was a hard way to make a living.

"I'll be praying for you, Darna," Millie promised as she hopped off the barstool. She had three minutes to make it to the bar area outside the casino for the trivia contest.

"Please don't tell anyone," Darna begged.

Millie turned around but didn't slow her pace. "Your secret is safe with me. With us," she pointed to Annette.

Annette made a zipping motion across her lips. "My lips are sealed."

Millie darted across the floor at a good clip. Annette hurried to keep up.

"I have two minutes to get to the casino area," Millie gasped.

"Take the stairs," Annette suggested.

Millie did just that. She power-walked to the stairs and then climbed them two at a time. It was two flights up to the casino. She made it in record-time, with a full minute to spare.

Beads of sweat popped out onto her forehead and she nervously wiped them away as she silently counted the crowd of people.

Annette sidestepped Millie. "You'll do fine," she whispered in her ear before heading to the kitchen.

Millie grabbed the pads of paper and pencils and handed them to the guests. She found the folder containing the answers tucked into a small cabinet in the wall next to the bar. She slid her glasses on and picked up the trivia list.

Halfway through the game, Millie relaxed. Andy stopped by to check on her and gave her the thumbs up after listening to her engage the crowd.

Several of the guests stopped by to chat after the trivia ended. They made a point to tell her it had been the most entertaining trivia game they had ever played. Millie was thrilled. She'd finally found her calling on board the ship. Trivia and solving mysteries.

She slid the trivia folder and pencils back in the cabinet and strolled down the hall, passing by the gift shop on her way to Andy's office. Millie glanced in the gift shop window as she passed by. The door was shut, but she could still see Cat inside. The shops and casino closed while the ship was in port.

Millie tapped the window and Cat motioned her inside. Cat's hair was in the same beehive style she'd had before except this time, she sported a bright yellow ribbon. Long locks of hair flowed down and rested on her shoulders.

She fixed her cat-green eyes on Millie. "I heard you're knee-deep in the Olivia LaShay murder case."

Cat dusted a glass penguin figurine before setting it back down.

Millie nodded. "There's no lack of motive, that's for sure."

"I would be careful if I were you," Cat warned. "There are a lot of people who think you're sticking your nose in where it doesn't belong."

"Like whom?" Millie asked.

Cat shrugged. "Just people. I don't want to name any names."

Millie changed the subject. "Have you found a replacement yet?"

Cat paused, duster in midair. Her green eyes narrowed. "As a matter of fact, Maribelle, Olivia's cabin mate, just took the job."

She turned her attention back to the display case. "It's a step up, you know. Moving from the wait staff to the stores. Plus, it's more money."

Millie was sure it was more money and not as tiresome of a job. There was more time off, especially since the stores closed while the ship was in port and more ports equaled more time off.

"Are you happy with the replacement?"

Cat nodded. "There'll be a lot less drama with Maribelle than there was with Olivia."

Millie didn't doubt that was true. She wasn't sure how anyone could have more drama than Olivia. That, and more boyfriends.

Millie wandered back to her room. She ticked off the list of suspects. First, of course, was Maribelle. She had motive and opportunity; but why would she leave such obvious evidence in her room? Then again, maybe it was the reverse psychology thing.

Then there was Andy. The fact that several people suspected him gave her reason to pause. She made a note to do a little research on the dead fiancé. What was her name? Gloria? No. That was her cousin's name. Aurora? No. That wasn't it, either.

She snapped her fingers. It was similar to her car, still parked in the garage at home. Crown Victoria. She had the first name down pat, and the last name. Dowry. No, it was similar to dowry. *Dowden.* That was it. Victoria Dowden.

Next on the list was Doctor Gundervan. He had lied and told Annette and her that he had never met Olivia. Millie suspected he was married. Maybe he and Olivia were having a fling and she was blackmailing him.

She scratched Darna off the list. Instead, she decided to add him to her prayer list.

Last, but not least, was Cat. The woman hadn't cared for Olivia. Still, she had the least motive, unless there was something more to it than Olivia telling people Cat was about to get fired and she (Olivia) was going to take her place.

Maybe Cat had a boyfriend and Olivia was after him, too. Another notch in her belt so to speak. She almost crossed her off the list but changed her mind. There was something about her...

She opened her cabin door with her room card, stepped inside and stepped on something that crunched under her shoe. It was a piece of paper. She bent down and picked it up.

The writing was small and Millie slipped on her glasses. *"The itsy bitsy spider crawled into Millie's room."*

Millie's heart began to pound. No one had ever threatened her before and this was definitely a threat.

Her eyes darted around the room as she checked for the slightest movement...spider moves. Was someone planning to place a deadly spider in her room?

Sarah arrived moments later to find Millie still holding the note and standing in the exact same spot. "What's wrong?"

Millie thrust the note in her direction. "Read this."

Sarah scanned the note and handed it back to Millie. "Where did you get this?"

"I found it right here." Millie pointed at the floor. "Someone shoved it under our door."

Millie tiptoed to her bunk and eased onto the edge, the note still in her hand.

"What are we going to do?" Sarah shuddered. "I think I'm gonna run out and get some bug spray."

The ship would be in port for several more hours, giving Sarah plenty of time to track down a can of insect spray.

"I'll go with you." Millie wanted to be anywhere but in that room.

The girls grabbed their backpacks and headed to the exit. It was a long hike from the ship to the shops. The heat was stifling as it radiated off the concrete dock.

Millie's scalp grew damp and her hair clung to her forehead. "It must be nearly a hundred degrees out here," she said as she swiped at the wisps of hair stuck to her brow.

"No kidding." Sarah stopped in her tracks. "Will ya' look at that." She pointed to a group of people directly ahead of them.

Millie shaded her eyes. It was hard to see through the haze of the Sahara-like heat. "Over there." Sarah pointed to a couple walking at a brisk pace. Although not quite touching, they were close together.

Millie didn't recognize them, at least not from the back. She frowned. "Who is it?"

"Donovan Sweeney and Alison Coulter," Sarah said.

Millie had met the tall blonde dancer on her first day. She was the girl with the legs that went on forever. Millie wasn't sure how she could've missed them, considering Alison was a head taller. "Wow. The staff on this ship is straight out of a soap opera."

The girls stopped inside the first gift shop they found. Millie's heart sank. The place not only didn't have bug spray, they didn't have a suggestion on where to find some.

"How can a tropical island not sell bug spray?" Sarah complained.

They continued to the next shop. Finally, four stores later, they found a small plastic container of insect repellant.

Sarah plucked it from the shelf and turned it over. "Seven dollars and seventy-nine cents for this tiny thing?"

Millie took it from her. "I'm buying it. After all, it's my fault we're here." Her eyes scanned the shelves. "Maybe we should buy some gas masks while we're at it."

Millie paid for the spray and the women stepped out of the shop and onto the sidewalk.

During the walk back to the ship, Millie was quiet, and Sarah correctly guessed it had everything to do with the note. She reached over and touched her arm. "Don't worry about it, Millie. I think it's just an empty threat. You should probably turn it into security though."

Millie nodded. If something happened to her, to them, authorities would know it wasn't an accident. She made a mental note to stay away from the railings.

Sarah headed to their room with the bug spray while Millie headed to the security office. She'd never had a reason to visit security. Of course, she'd only been on the ship a couple of days.

She followed the placard on the wall, down a long corridor until she reached the very end and a door marked, *Security*.

Millie suddenly realized it wasn't far from the infirmary and Doctor Gundervan's office. She turned the knob and stepped inside.

At first, Millie thought the room was empty until she heard a small shuffling noise coming from the back. "Hello?"

"Be right there," a muffled male voice echoed from the back.

Millie glanced around the small room as she waited. There were several plaques on the wall. She leaned in and squinted her eyes as she studied the name, *Dave Patterson*. In the corner of the frame was a picture of a smiling man, who looked to be about her age. "Can I help you?"

Millie nearly jumped out of her skin as she swung around and came face-to-face with the bluest eyes she had ever seen. She swallowed nervously. "I-I uh..."

The corners of his eyes crinkled kindly.

She tried again. "Yes. Uh..." Millie wished she could turn around and kick herself. She was mumbling like an idiot. "Yes, I'm Millie Sanders, Assistant Cruise Director." She tugged at the corner of her damp shirt.

"Ah. The infamous Millie." The man settled into a chair and motioned to one on the other side. "You're trying to steal my job," he teased.

"I am?" Millie squeaked.

He shook his head. "That's okay. I don't mind."

"So to what do I owe the pleasure of this visit?"

Millie fumbled with the zipper on her backpack. The man was completely unnerving her.

She pulled the folded note from her bag and slid it across the desk. "I found this in my cabin earlier. Someone shoved it under my door."

The smile disappeared as he pulled a pair of reading glasses from the desk drawer and slipped them on. He unfolded the note and read the words.

His eyes narrowed as he gazed at her over the rim of his glasses. "You have any idea who might've left this?"

Millie shook her head. "None."

He folded the note and set if off to the side. "I'll need to keep this for evidence," he told her.

She nodded. "Of course."

He folded his hands and placed them on top of the desk. "I suppose I don't have to tell you to be careful."

"Yeah. Like stay away from railings and check for hairy insects..." The words were out of her mouth before she realized it sounded dumb, at least it did to her. As if the killer would try that route again. "I.

We - my roommate Sarah and I - bought some bug spray."

He nodded. "Not a bad idea." Patterson studied the woman across from him. He was a good judge of character and he liked her. Although she seemed a little nervous, he could tell she had a bit of spunk in her. Of course, he'd heard the rumors of how she was sticking her nose in where it didn't belong.

He leaned forward and studied the woman across from him. Wisps of hair framed her face. Her brown eyes, filled with concern, met his.

He gave a mental shake. *Earth to Dave.* "How's your investigation going? Any suspects?"

"Yeah," she admitted. "Olivia had plenty of enemies. so there are a lot of suspects."

He grabbed the pen on his desk and began twirling it around in circles. "Care to tell me who you think they are?"

"You mean you don't have your *own*?"

What kind of security / detective person was he if he didn't have his own list of suspects? She wondered.

He cut her off. "Of course I do."

"I'm sorry Detective. Officer..."

"It's Officer Patterson. I'm a retired police officer from the State of Florida," he explained.

Millie nodded. "Officer Patterson. Well, my list is long." She told him about Cat, about Maribelle and Robert, Maribelle's boyfriend. She also mentioned Zack, but added that she didn't really consider him a suspect.

She almost mentioned Andy, but thought that bordered betrayal. Instead, she bit her lip. "That's all."

Dave's eyes narrowed. "What about your boss, Andy?"

Millie's eyes dropped as she studied her hands. "Yeah, he might be a suspect, too," she admitted.

Her head shot up. "I almost forgot one. Doctor Gundervan."

Patterson lifted a brow. "Really?"

She told him how he had lied and told Annette and Millie that he hadn't known Olivia LaShay yet they knew for a fact that wasn't true.

He tapped the pen on the desk. "That's interesting."

Millie glanced at the clock. "I have to go or I'll be late." She didn't wait for him to reply as she bolted out of the office and sprinted down the hall, her backpack bobbing up and down as she ran.

Patterson stepped over to the open door. He gazed down the hall in the direction Millie had taken and watched until she was out of sight before slowly closing the door, the smile never leaving his face.

Chapter 10

Millie dashed up the four flights of stairs to the deck where passengers were returning to the ship. Andy was standing by the entrance, greeting the guests. She slipped in beside him and smoothed her hair.

"A minute and a half. You're getting better," he joked.

"Either that, or I'm getting faster at sprinting."

She stood next to Andy and greeted the weary, but smiling guests. They all looked relaxed, happy and tired. All of them except for a young family who rushed forward. The man was holding the arm of a young girl. "My daughter was stung by a bee and is having trouble breathing."

Millie's eyes darted to the girl's flushed face. She knew in an instant that the young girl was having an allergic reaction. "She needs to get to medical." Millie didn't wait for an answer as she grabbed the young girl's arm and pulled her to the nearest elevator where several people were waiting to board.

"Medical emergency. Please stand aside."

The crowd stepped back as the young girl and her family rushed inside the open elevator.

Millie unclipped her radio from her belt and switched the radio to the emergency channel. "This is Millie Sanders. I need Doctor Gundervan STAT!" she shouted.

The line crackled for a moment as Millie prayed.

"This is Doctor Gundervan."

"Yes, I am in the elevator headed to medical. We have a young guest who may be having an allergic reaction." She sucked in a breath and waited for what seemed like an eternity.

Finally, he replied. "I'll meet you there."

When the elevator doors opened, Millie wrapped her arm around the girl's shoulder and propelled her forward. The girl had taken a turn for the worse as she began to wheeze and gasp for air. "We're almost there. Hang on."

Doctor Gundervan was waiting outside the door. He opened it wide and the family rushed in. He took one look at the young girl, reached behind him and grabbed a syringe as he glanced at the man. "Does she have any allergies?"

"No."

Doctor Gundervan lifted the girl's sleeve and injected the needle. The girl swayed back and forth.

Within seconds, the girl's pinched expression relaxed, her breathing returned to normal and she smiled. "I feel much better now."

Millie drew a shaky breath. She felt like bursting into tears.

"You'll need to stay here for observation for a while," Doctor Gundervan told her.

Her job complete, Millie turned to go.

The girl's mother stopped her before she walked out the door. She grabbed Millie's hand and squeezed it tight. "Thank you so much for saving my daughter," she said.

Millie blinked back the tears that filled her eyes. "I-I." She was about to say, "I didn't do anything" but instead she simply said, "You're welcome."

When she returned to the gangway, Andy gave her a sideways glance. "Aren't you the jack of all trades? Trivia queen, life saver, not to mention amateur sleuth." The smile faded. "In all seriousness, you may have saved that young girl's life."

Millie swallowed the lump in her throat and gave him a watery smile before turning her attention to the guests. For the second time that day, she had almost started crying in front of her boss.

Andy and she stayed near the entrance until the last guest boarded and security shut the door. "I'm heading up to the theater to check on tonight's show. We have another trivia at seven o'clock by the casino bar if you'd like to run with it."

Millie nodded. The last one had been a blast. "You bet."

He nodded approvingly. "It's almost dinner time. Why don't you go eat, then make a run up to the lido deck to check on the sail away party."

She gave him a mock salute. "Yes, sir."

He rolled his eyes. "Now get out of here before I change my mind and make you emcee the show tonight."

Millie's eyes widened in horror. That was the last thing she wanted to do. Before Andy could change his mind, she spun around and headed to her preferred method of getting around the ship - the stairs. It was good exercise and it left more space on the elevators for the guests.

The buffet's dinner theme was, "A Taste of the Islands." Millie skipped the salad this time. Instead, she grabbed a tray and started down the line. She picked up a conch fritter, jerk chicken, some sticky rice and crusty rolls. Her mouth began to water at the tantalizing smells.

She carefully balanced her tray, making a pit stop at the beverage station for a watered down iced tea. After she filled her glass, she gazed around the dining room. There, in the far corner of the cafeteria, was Annette. She spied Millie at the same time.

Millie slid her overflowing tray onto the table and pulled out a chair. "What's that?"

Annette peeled the wrapper from the straw and shoved it in her glass. "What's what?"

"This?" Annette picked up a yellow-ish disc and took a big bite. "Fried plantain. They only serve this one night per cruise. I think I'm addicted to them."

Millie picked up her fork and gazed at the plantain. "Hmm." They were nothing that interested her.

Annette unfolded her napkin and placed it in her lap. "I heard you found some kind of mysterious note in your cabin."

Millie's eyebrows shot up. News traveled fast around the ship. "Someone is trying to scare me off the investigation."

Annette nibbled the edge of the plantain. "You're not gonna give up, are you?" Millie was the most exciting thing that had happened on the ship in eons. That and the murder, of course.

Millie stiffened her back. "Of course not." She picked up a jerk chicken wing and took a bite. The veiled threat was going to backfire. If anything, it made her even more determined to find the murderer.

Chapter 11

The sail away party was in full swing by the time Millie made it topside. Zack Smythe was smack dab in the center of all the action as he led throngs of passengers in a rousing rendition of Macarena. It looked like fun. Millie grinned at Zack, who gave her a quick wink as she headed over to the railing.

She glanced around nervously, a fleeting thought that someone might be getting ready to bum-rush her and push her over the side ran through her mind.

The ship was slipping away from the dock. Millie peered down the long side at the passengers who were doing exactly what she was doing.

Off in the distance she heard a loud shriek.

Racing along the dock was a portly woman, holding onto a wide brimmed floppy hat and clomping along in a pair of flip-flops. She held an empty drink glass in her other hand and was frantically waving it back and forth as she shouted at the ship to come back.

One of the passengers standing next to Millie started to chuckle. "Looks like twinkles missed the boat. Literally."

Millie inched closer. "Twinkles?"

"That's what we nicknamed her. She was in Tiki Time doing shots when we left. Life of the party, that one," he added.

Tiki Time was a resort bar a short walk from the dock. Millie and Sarah had passed by it earlier, on their way back to the ship.

Millie turned her attention to the poor woman, who was now standing near the water's edge. She prayed she wouldn't do anything stupid like dive into the water and start swimming out.

She didn't. Instead, she flopped onto the concrete, face down. Millie wished she had a bag of popcorn. This was better than the movies.

The woman lay motionless on the ground. *Maybe she passed out.* Millie let out the breath she'd been holding as she watched a golf cart pull up next to the woman.

A man in uniform jumped out of the driver's side. He leaned over the woman and gently shook her shoulder. She didn't even flinch.

A second man, wearing a security guard uniform and seated in the passenger seat, joined him. He kneeled over the woman and shook her, all the while shouting in her ear. The wind carried his voice. "Wake up, Sleeping Beauty."

That got the crowd going. The spectators began to chant "Beauty! Beauty!" Finally, the woman came to enough to roll over on her back.

The men each grabbed hold of her arms and half-carried, half-dragged the woman to the back of the golf cart where they unceremoniously dropped her on the bench seat.

The driver got behind the wheel as the guard in the passenger side reached back and grabbed onto the woman's arm to keep her from falling out.

The crowd cheered as the golf cart made a sharp U-turn, sending the passengers careening to the right before the driver stomped on the gas and the cart raced off toward the island.

Millie had to wonder what the cost of missing the cruise ship might be. She hoped she never had to find out.

The party on lido was in full swing as the steel drum band began to play and passengers joined in the festivities. Millie wandered around the lido deck, smiling at guests and picking up a cup here or a plate there along the way.

She glanced down at her watch. Trivia started in half an hour. Determined to be early for a change, she dropped the dishes in the bins and headed back indoors.

She couldn't wait to find out the trivia theme. She hoped it was something she was good at. Several guests had already gathered in chairs near the trivia area and she recognized some of them from the 70's game.

Using her key to unlock the cabinet, she reached inside to pull out the manila folder with the questions and several pads of paper along with a pack of pencils.

She slid her glasses on her nose and peered down at the question and answer sheet. Her heart skipped a beat as she read the top of the sheet and the trivia questions: *Twenty of the Deadliest Insects in the World.*

Her eyes narrowed as she cast a suspicious glance around the room. She wondered if this was some kind of sick joke or maybe another veiled threat.

Millie set her lips in a straight line. Millie Sanders was no coward. If this was someone's attempt to intimidate her, it was going to backfire.

When seven o'clock rolled around, Millie grabbed the microphone and switched it to on. "Did everyone have a fun day in Nassau?" The crowd cheered.

She pushed the nagging thought that someone watching her wished her harm - and smiled. "Good. Good. How many of you went on an excursion?" she asked.

The majority of the participants raised their hands.

Millie was really getting into this entertainment-thing. "How 'bout sweating off a couple pounds in the heat?"

All the hands were back up. Millie grinned. "Yeah, it was a hot one. Today's trivia isn't for the faint of heart. It's all about creepy-crawlies and some of the deadliest insects in the world so get your pencil and paper ready. Here we go."

Millie made the game a fun one, even though it was the oddest trivia she had ever seen. Only one of the guests came close - with twenty-four of the twenty-five questions answered. Interestingly enough, the one Millie missed was a fact about a rare and deadly spider.

"Gotta watch out for those spiders," she joked. "You never know when one of them is gonna show up." *Or someone is going to try to take you out with one.*

She shoved the manila folder back in the cabinet. "Take that," she mumbled under her breath.

"You have a real knack for trivia." Andy snuck up behind her and handed her the packet of pencils. Millie set the packet on the shelf, locked the cabinet and turned to face him. "So far this is one of my favorite parts of the job. It doesn't even seem like work."

Andy smiled at a couple passing by. "Heard about some kind of threatening note you found in your cabin."

His jaw tightened and he locked eyes with Millie. "You're the new kid on the block, Millie. Don't start off on the wrong foot, ruffling feathers."

Millie sucked in a breath and nodded. "You're right."

He draped his arm across her shoulders and gave her a gentle shake. "Even I can't resist a good mystery," he admitted. "Just be careful, Millie. That's all."

Millie let out the breath she'd been holding. It was as if he was giving her the go-ahead to continue her investigation. She watched as he headed down the long corridor and then disappeared down the steps that led to the lower level of the casino.

Millie wasn't in Kansas anymore, or in her case - Michigan. She pondered the case as she walked back to her cabin. She had no one to trust, not even Annette. There was a killer roaming free and she was determined to figure out who that was.

Chapter 12

Millie's eyes shot open. For a moment, she couldn't remember where she was, and then it dawned on her. She was in the middle of the ocean...on a cruise ship.

She threw the covers aside and dangled her legs over the edge. There were times she still wondered what on earth had possessed her to take a job on a cruise ship. A moment - or moments - of temporary insanity.

It had taken Millie a while to fall asleep the night before. She kept feeling as if something were crawling on her.

She stumbled into the bathroom, flipped the light switch on and peered into the mirror. Her hair stuck out in every direction and looked as if it had been caught up in a whirlwind.

Millie had placed a clean uniform under the sink the night before. She quickly showered and slipped into a pair of Bermuda shorts and work shirt, which was a welcome relief from the long pants that she was required to wear on the ship.

Today was different. Today was the day they stopped at the cruise line's private island, *South Seas Cay*. Millie had never visited a private island before and she was excited to see it.

Andy had assigned her shore duty, and although Millie didn't care much for the heat, she would rather be on the island than on the ship. She wanted her feet to hit dry land, at least once in a while.

Her boss explained to her that she needed to be on the first shuttle boat to shore since she would be in charge of helping set up the island activities. Some of the activities included a volleyball match, which sounded too much like work, and a limbo contest, which was *definitely* not Millie's thing.

The boat ride was quick and Millie was one of the first ones off. She traipsed across the sand toward the beach area.

Although her shirt was white and the fabric cotton, for which she was extremely grateful, the hot Caribbean sun beat down on her head. Soon, she was sweating from head to toe.

Darna, the bartender and Olivia's brother, caught a glimpse of her struggling to assemble the volleyball nets and rushed over. "You look like you could use some help." He handed her a towel. "Thanks." She wiped her brow and hung it on the net.

With Darna's help, the two of them managed to wiggle the posts in place. After they finished, they headed for the nearest palm tree.

One of the bartenders passed by, carrying a tray of bottled waters. Darna snagged two and handed one to Millie. She unscrewed the cap and took a big gulp. She wiped her mouth with the back of her hand and gazed at Darna.

He chugged his water and screwed the top back on the empty container. "I heard someone left you a threatening note."

Millie nodded. News sure did travel fast around the ship.

"What did the note look like?"

"It was about this big." Millie held out her fingers. "And it was pale blue."

He gazed out at the turquoise waters and nodded. "That's the stuff the ship's officer's use. Medical staff, the captain. You know, the upper echelon."

"Huh." Millie stuck a hand on her hip. *Medical staff...as in Doctor Gundervan.*

"Of course, anyone could lift a sheet of paper on the ship. It wouldn't be hard to do." Darna nodded at something behind Millie. "Wonder what he's doing onshore."

Millie followed his gaze. Doctor Gundervan stood next to a row of lounge chairs, talking to Maribelle, Olivia's former roommate. Their heads were close together and they were having what she guessed was a serious conversation.

"I don't trust her," Darna told Millie.

Millie didn't trust her, either. Of course, at this point she didn't trust anyone. She gave Darna a quick glance. What if he had killed his sister? After all, he was around her more than anyone else was.

A shiver ran down her spine despite the unbearable heat.

"Be careful of heat stroke," he warned. "Tis easy to do. I better get back to work."

Darna headed to his workstation, a covered tiki bar.

She stood there for another long moment watching Maribelle and the good ole' doctor chat it up before she trudged across the sand and headed to the food stations to check on the progress.

Motive and opportunity. That's what ran through Millie's mind. The two went together. When she could figure out who not only had motive, but also the perfect opportunity, she would have the killer.

The rest of the afternoon flew by. More than once, she wished she were one of the guests wearing a bikini, lounging under a palm tree and sipping a fruity drink. Well, maybe not the bikini part, but definitely the lounging under a palm tree part with a frosty drink in hand.

Millie was on the last shuttle and one of the last to return to the ship. She had worked her tail off and had been so busy that she'd only had time to grab a small roast beef slider in between tasks. She began to feel nauseous from lack of food as the boat chugged across the open water.

She could see Darna hanging out in the back, talking to Alison Coulter, the blonde dancer. Alison tipped her head back and laughed at something Darna said to her.

Millie thought they made a cute couple. She wondered if they were dating. Then she remembered that Donovan Sweeney, the purser, and Alison had gotten off the ship together in Nassau.

Millie shook her head. *This place had more drama than Days of Our Lives.*

Back in the cabin, Millie stripped off her sweaty clothes and climbed into the shower. She turned the water on cold and stood there for several long moments, letting the cool water pelt her sore, tired muscles.

By the time she finished showering and changed, she felt better. Andy had given her the rest of the evening off since she'd worked the entire day without a single break.

Millie slipped into clean clothes and opened the cabin door to head topside. There, standing on the other side of the door, was Annette.

She looked as if she was about to explode. "I have a brilliant idea." Annette exclaimed. She grabbed Millie's arm and dragged her back into the room before slamming the door shut behind them.

Millie didn't have the heart to tell her she was about to pass out from hunger. Instead, she plopped down on the edge of the bed as Annette slid into the only chair. "We need a stakeout."

Millie's brow shot up. "A stakeout?"

"A stakeout to flush out the killer."

"Why didn't I think of that?"

"Too much heat today, I reckon," Annette teased. "Listen, here's my plan. We spread the word that you have evidence you're about to turn over to Patterson."

Annette paused. "I heard you two had a cozy little visit."

Millie's mouth dropped open. "Why, I..."

Annette waved a hand. "Now, I'm not one to gossip, so don't worry about me."

Millie closed her mouth and gave Annette a dark look.

Annette rambled on with ideas about the stakeout while Millie's mind wandered. First, she was a "busybody," then someone was sending her threatening notes and now she was "getting cozy" with Detective Patterson.

And she hadn't even been on the ship for a week.

"...so we let it slip that you have incriminating evidence," Annette continued.

Millie shook her head. "I'm sorry, Annette. I missed that last part." Actually, she had missed almost all of it.

"I was just saying that we tell them you stumbled on some evidence and it's hidden in your cabin."

"How do we catch them in the act?"

Annette jumped to her feet. "Follow me." She opened Millie's bathroom door and climbed up on the bathroom counter.

Above the counter was an access panel Millie had never noticed.

Annette popped the panel off, shoved it to the side and looked down at Millie. "Give me a boost."

Millie stepped inside and grabbed the bottom of Annette's sneaker, giving it a shove and hoisting Annette up through the panel and into the ceiling.

"I don't get a warm fuzzy about this," Millie warned.

"Don't worry, I've done this before," Annette's muffled voice echoed from the opening.

The ceiling tiles shifted as Millie watched Annette shimmy across the bathroom ceiling and into the small cabin.

She squeezed her eyes shut certain that at any second Annette would come crashing through. Millie had no idea how she could explain that.

"I'm over here."

Millie followed the voice to a small, square vent in the center of the cabin and looked up. She could see Annette's piercing eyes through the vent holes.

"I can hide in here and wait for whoever it is to show up."

Millie liked the idea. The only part she didn't like was that she hadn't thought of it. "Were you a detective in another life?" Millie teased.

"No. Let's just say I had an interesting career years ago. Plus, I love to watch old re-runs of Murder, We Wrote."

Millie waited for Annette to crawl back out of the ceiling before replacing the panel and wiping the dust off the counter. The lightheaded sensation returned. "I'm going to grab a bite to eat. You wanna join me?"

Annette swiped at her pant legs. "I can't. I need to head back up to the kitchen and work on tomorrow's dinner menu. I have to have it on paper for the sous chef. If not," she made a slicing motion across her neck, "it's off with my head."

Millie followed Annette down the corridor and into the passenger area. They climbed the steps and stopped in front of the entrance to the galley.

"I'll work on spreading the word." Annette winked at Millie and disappeared behind the door.

Dinner in the dining room was in full swing, which meant that there would be few passengers in the buffet area; something Millie was starting to enjoy.

She loved the passengers, loved their excitement, but there were moments it was good to get away from it all.

Millie made a beeline for the burger station. She had been tortured all day with the smells of grilling hamburgers and hotdogs. She grabbed a tray and headed to the order window.

Catherine, "Cat" slipped in behind her, tray in hand. "I hear you're quite the busybody around here." She grabbed a bundle of silverware from the towering stack nearby.

Millie groaned inwardly and stepped in front of the window as she smiled at the young man behind the counter. "I'll take a cheeseburger with extra cheese."

She turned to Cat, still standing beside her. "What's that supposed to mean?"

Cat grabbed a fry from her plate and chewed thoughtfully. "Just that you're determined to solve Olivia's murder and that you've been hanging out in Patterson's office."

Millie clenched her fist. "I am *not* hanging out in Patterson's office," she gritted out.

Cat raised an eyebrow. "My, my. A little defensive, aren't we?"

Millie didn't answer. Her burger was ready. "Thank you." She turned on her heel and without uttering another syllable to Cat, walked the other way.

She made a quick stop at the dessert station where she grabbed a piece of strawberry pie on her way to a corner table. As far away from people - and Cat - as possible. She set the tray on the table and unwrapped her silverware before reaching for the bottle of ketchup.

"We meet again. Do you mind if I sit here?"

Millie shrugged her shoulders, determined not to let Cat see how she was getting under her skin. "Help yourself," she muttered.

Cat settled in the chair across from her. Millie watched as she shifted her plates from the tray to the table. Maybe eating with Cat wasn't such a bad idea. It would give her a chance to find out a little more information about Olivia and her enemies.

Millie set her plate and pie on the table and placed the empty tray on the seat next to her.

Cat already thought Millie was a snoop, so there was no point in beating around the bush. "Olivia sure had her share of enemies."

Cat patted the tip of her beehive hairdo and lifted her burger. "It would be easier to list the people that did like her."

"What about Darna?"

"There was something odd about those two. They were always together and Darna never seemed to mind when Olivia flirted with other men."

Millie sipped her water thoughtfully. Apparently, Cat wasn't aware that Darna and Olivia were brother and sister. *What if Darna had lied to Millie? What if he and Olivia weren't related and he made it up to throw Millie off?*

She made a mental note to see if she could verify the accuracy of his confession.

Cat took a big bite of burger and studied Millie. "I would put Andy on the list."

Cat leaned forward. "Your boss. Andy," she whispered. "He had the hots for Olivia and she scorned him. Publicly embarrassed him, really."

Millie was all ears. "Go on."

"The day before she died, they had some sort of spat in front of Kids Korner." "Kids Korner" was an activity center for the junior passengers. Millie had walked by it a couple of times, but had never gone inside to check it out.

She remembered Andy telling her that his fiancé had died years ago. Could Andy be a killer?

Cat had also mentioned Toby, the former assistant cruise director. Maybe she was jealous since, in Millie's opinion, being assistant cruise director was a better job than running the ship's store, which meant Cat probably didn't care for Millie that much, either.

It was probably best that she keep Cat at arm's length and not share too much information with her until she was certain she could be trusted.

"...has a photo of Olivia lying on the floor in the atrium." Cat was still talking.

Millie, deep in thought, had missed what she said. "Who has a photo of Olivia?"

Cat rolled her eyes. "No, I was just saying that Donovan Sweeney took pictures of Olivia's body. I watched him."

Donovan Sweeney was the ship's purser. She didn't know him that well, but she intended to change that ASAP. She wanted to see those photos.

Maribelle sauntered over with a tray of food just as Millie was finishing hers. Maribelle sat and Millie stood. It was the perfect opportunity to make a hasty retreat.

"It has been a long day. I think I'll turn in." Millie didn't wait for a reply as she picked up her empty plates and headed toward the exit.

She dropped her dirty dishes in the bin next to the sliding doors and made a beeline for the guest services desk in hopes that Donovan was working the late shift.

She made a quick trip down several flights of stairs until she reached deck five. Her eyes scanned the long gleaming counter until she caught a glimpse of Donovan standing near the half door on the far right side of the counter.

It appeared that he was getting ready to leave.

Millie made fast tracks to the counter just as Donovan stepped to the other side. "Millie Sanders. I heard you're doing a great job and even managed to avert a medical crisis of one of our pint-size passengers."

Millie's face warmed. She had become so wrapped up in the investigation, she had almost forgotten about the girl and the bee sting. "It was nothing."

"You're being too modest," Donovan replied.

"I heard you snapped a couple pictures of Olivia before her body was covered and taken away."

Donovan's eyes narrowed as he stared at Millie for a long second. "I did."

Millie wilted under his gaze. It was now or never. "I was wondering if I might take a peek at those pictures."

"The company has a team of investigators on the case now." He shook his head. "Are you that bored with your job? I'm sure Andy can find more to keep you busy."

"No, not at all." Millie loved her job, but this was personal, as if she had something to prove. To

Roger. Not that it would matter. Why would he care if she were in the middle of the ocean solving mysteries? He was probably happy she was thousands of miles away.

"It gives me a purpose, a reason to get up in the morning." Sudden tears burned the back of her eyes.

Donovan reached out and touched her hand. "I'm sorry, Millie. I didn't mean to upset you. Let's go." Millie hadn't meant to play on his sympathies, but it looked like that had done the trick.

Millie followed him up the stairs and onto the promenade deck.

"Over there." He pointed to a long metal bench.

After they sat down, Donovan pulled out his cell phone and turned it on. He flipped through the screen and then handed the phone to Millie.

The body was exactly how Millie remembered seeing it that day on the floor in front of the bar. She studied the photo carefully and scrolled to the next one.

There were several more photos and some of them included people who had gathered around the woman's body.

She recognized Robert, the bartender. Robert was the one who was dating Maribelle.

In another photo was Andy and someone Millie could swear was Alison Coulter, the blonde dancer, but the woman's head was turned to the side and she couldn't be a hundred percent certain.

There was one more person that showed up in a couple of the pictures. It was a man and someone who worked on board the ship because he was wearing a lanyard, although she could see that he wasn't wearing a uniform.

Millie held up the phone. "Who is that?"

Donovan tilted his head as he studied the photo. "That's Toby Oglesby, the former assistant cruise director."

He continued. "He must've been on his way out when this picture was taken."

Millie nodded. She had never seen a picture of Toby before. She remembered that someone had mentioned he had a crush on Olivia.

Millie studied the photos one more time and then handed the phone back to Donovan. "Thanks for showing the pictures to me."

Donovan slipped the phone in his front pants pocket. "I didn't care for Olivia all that much either. She wasn't a nice person, but she didn't deserve to die."

He paused as they watched a young couple stroll past. He gave a small nod and waited until they were out of earshot. "Dave Patterson harbored an intense dislike for Olivia, too."

Chapter 13

Millie turned startled eyes to Donovan. The fact that Detective Patterson didn't like Olivia shouldn't have come as a surprise. It seemed like the only people on the ship who liked her either were dating her or related to her.

The list of suspects was growing by the minute. At this rate, she would never be able to figure out who killed Olivia, unless she went with Annette's idea to set up some sort of sting. It was beginning to look like their only viable option.

She didn't mention the sting to Donovan. He was on the list of suspects, too.

She thanked him again for his time and stood. She wanted to head back to the cabin to mull over the new information.

As she wound her way around the ship, she focused on the killer's weapon - the spider. Someone had to have noticed the spider and small terrarium somewhere along the way. The killer had to sneak the spider on board, which meant they would have purchased it in port.

She snapped her fingers and glanced at her watch. Annette was off the clock now. If she was lucky, Millie could catch up with her in the galley.

When she reached the galley, she stood on her tiptoes and peeked in through the large, round window. She let out a sigh of relief when she spied the top of Annette's dark head as she moved back and forth.

"I'm glad you're still here."

"I'm all wound up about the stakeout, so I thought I'd come down here and whip up some treats for my crew," Annette said.

Millie eyed the counter, covered in baking supplies. "What're you making?"

"A good ole apple crisp."

Millie stepped closer. "Can I help?"

Annette placed a large bag of honey crisp apples on the counter. She pulled a knife from the rack and set it next to the bag. "You can slice the apples if you want."

Millie rolled up her sleeves and headed to the sink to wash her hands. After her hands were clean, she pulled an apron over her head and tied the strings in the back. She lifted a large, glass bowl from under the counter and set it next to the bag.

Annette measured the sugars and flour while Millie began slicing the apples. "I was thinking about the spider...the one that killed Olivia." She sliced the apple into thin pieces and tossed the pieces in the bottom of the bowl. "The killer must have somehow gotten the spider while in port."

Annette scooped a measured cup of softened butter and scraped it into the bowl. "True."

"I'm just thinking out loud, but it makes sense that they would've done it just before killing Olivia, so there would be less chance that someone would discover the spider. I would think it would be hard to hide something like that."

Annette added nutmeg and cinnamon to the mixture and picked up a fork. "I hadn't thought about that."

"So I was wondering," Millie said, "what port did the ship stop in just before it docked in Miami? The day Olivia died."

"Let me think. That would've been Jamaica." Annette began stirring the mixture. "We weren't in port for very long, maybe four or so hours, which wouldn't give the killer much time to track down a spider."

Millie picked up where Annette left off. "Which means that it was close to port and a place we might be able to find."

The women finished the sentence together: "and we'll be in Jamaica day after tomorrow."

Annette began to ramble. "Oh my gosh, Millie. We need to see if we can track down whoever sells spiders."

The wheels in Millie's head were spinning ninety miles an hour. "We'll need pictures. You know, pictures of the suspects so we can take them around to show store owners."

Annette grabbed a measuring spoon and shook the end at Millie. "I have the perfect plan on how to get those pictures. We'll work on it in the morning."

"How about a little Christian music?" Annette didn't wait for an answer as she reached under the cabinet and pulled out a small portable radio.

Millie smiled when she caught Annette's eye. It was nice to have a trusted friend, someone she could talk to and who loved the Lord. It reminded her of a Bible verse:

"The righteous choose their friends carefully, but the way of the wicked leads them astray." Proverbs 12:26 NIV

Two heads were better than one. That was Millie's motto.

By the time the women finished the crisps and left them on the stainless steel counter to cool, it was after midnight and Millie was whupped. She had promised Andy she would meet him in his office bright and early the next morning to go over the day's schedule of events.

A ship day at sea meant that there would be a full day of activities scheduled to keep the passengers entertained. Not that she minded. Millie would rather be busy than sit around twiddling her thumbs.

Chapter 14

The next morning, Millie was up and ready to go. She knocked on Andy's cabin door at precisely 6:50 a.m., a solid ten minutes ahead of schedule.

The door swung open and Andy, who was already dressed for the day, grinned at Millie. "Ten minutes ahead of schedule. By George, I think you've got this timing thing down pat."

Millie beamed as she stepped inside the room. "I hoped you would notice."

Andy motioned for her to have a seat across from his. This was the first time Millie had ever been inside Andy's cabin. They usually met in his office behind the stage.

Millie was a bit envious of the size of his cabin, which was all his now that Toby was gone. If Millie had been a man, they would've shared the cabin.

She briefly wondered if that was one of the reasons he'd chosen a female - so he could have the space to himself.

There were tidy rows of papers spread out across the work surface. She listened as Andy mapped out the strategy for the day. She had to admire his level of organization. He had the day planned, right down to the very last event, the midnight chocolate extravaganza.

Millie's mouth watered at the thought of all the delectable sweet treats.

After going over the schedule, Andy grabbed one of the stacks and handed it to Millie. "These are your assignments. Do you think you can handle it?"

Millie nodded eagerly. Not only had he given her the trivia contest, she was in charge of bingo, which she loved to play and the galley tours, which would give her the perfect opportunity to meet up with Annette later.

She remembered the plan Annette and she had hatched the night before and that she needed to make excuses to take photos of the suspects. Millie whipped her cell phone out of her front pocket. "I was wondering if I could take a picture of you, to send home to my children."

Andy leaned back in his chair and ran a hand through his sparse red locks. "I suppose."

Millie lifted the phone and snapped his picture. She took one more picture, but didn't dare push for a third. She quickly turned the phone off and shoved it in her pocket.

She shifted uncomfortably and realized the several cups of coffee she'd consumed hit bottom. "Do you mind if I use your bathroom?"

"No. Go right ahead."

Millie slipped inside the bathroom and flipped the light on. The room was full of men's grooming items. A razor, some shave cream, a jar of

Brylcreem. She lifted the jar and inspected the front. She hadn't seen Brylcreem in years.

She carefully set the jar back down and lifted the toilet seat. The bathroom was larger than the one she shared with Sarah, although not by much.

She finished her business, flushed the toilet and then turned on the faucet. Out of the corner of her eye, something caught her attention. It was a set of medicine cabinets, something Sarah and she didn't have.

Millie dried her hands and gently tugged on the corner of the door. It swung silently open.

She admired the ample interior space for several seconds and started to close the door when something caught her eye. Millie stuck her hand inside and felt around. She grabbed the item and lifted it out. It was a wallet.

Millie knew she should put it back, but she couldn't help herself. Something told her to check the inside. Her fingers fumbled inside the compartments as she felt around. There was a slip of paper tucked in the very bottom of the last compartment. She slid the paper out and unfolded the sheet. It was a receipt. She didn't have her reading glasses and the letters were blurry.

"K---ston Pet -----." Her heart began to flutter. *Could this be a receipt for a pet store?*

She heard a commotion coming from outside the door. *Andy must wonder what on earth she was doing in his bathroom.* She quickly pulled her phone from her pocket, switched it on and snapped a photo.

Her fingers fumbled as she shoved the receipt back inside and placed the wallet in the cabinet. She quietly closed the cabinet door and took a deep breath.

Millie stepped out of the bathroom and clutched her stomach. "Gotta watch those spicy chicken wings," she moaned.

Andy was at a loss for words. Almost. "I hope you're alright."

"I'll be okay." She pointed to the bathroom. "I'm sorry about your bathroom."

Andy's eyes darted to the door. "I-I'll be sure to give it a little time to...clear out."

Millie grabbed her stack of papers. "I better head over to the gym and make sure the girls are ready for the early riser's yoga class." She patted the radio clipped to her belt. "Call me if you need me."

She spent the rest of the day working through her schedule. Despite the hectic pace, she was able to get pictures of everyone on her suspect list. Everyone that is, except for Cat. Every time she stopped by the gift shop, the place was packed. It didn't help that they were having their famous "gold-by-the-inch" sale.

Millie watched the throngs of people milling about. She rolled her eyes as two women elbowed each other at the fifty percent off table. *You would think they were giving the stuff away.*

She had barely enough time to grab a sandwich in between events and it was now just after seven o'clock. The main show in the theater was in full swing, which gave Millie a chance to wander upstairs to the buffet.

Tonight's themed dinner was All-American and Millie's favorite food. She eased a slice of pepperoni pizza on her plate, along with a hot dog, a generous helping of potato salad and a large scoop of coleslaw. On her way out, she grabbed a small serving of apple crisp that looked vaguely familiar.

Her mouth watered as she balanced the heavy tray and searched for a quiet corner. She spied

Annette's familiar brown head, her back turned toward her.

Millie picked up the pace and zigzagged across the room. "Hey, stranger."

Annette whirled around, a piece of ham and cheese pizza halfway to her mouth. Her eyebrows shot up as she glanced at Millie's stacked tray.

"I'm starving."

Annette pointed at the hot dog, loaded with onions, catsup, mustard and chili sauce. "Where did you get that?"

"Over there." Millie nodded in the direction she'd just come from as she unfolded her napkin and set it in her lap. "You'll never guess what happened today."

She pulled her phone from her pocket and turned it on. She slipped her glasses on and scrolled to the picture she had taken of the piece of paper she found in the wallet in Andy's bathroom cabinet.

"I found this in Andy's bathroom." She handed the phone to Annette.

Annette peered at it through the bottom of her glasses. "Kingston Pet Store, Kingston, Jamaica. Andy is the killer," she whispered.

"We'll find out tomorrow, after we track down this pet store and show them Andy's picture."

***

Millie was so depressed at the thought that Andy was Olivia's killer; she couldn't even muster a level of enthusiasm for the *Chocolate Extravaganza*. All she could do was wonder how such a nice man could be a killer. She remembered his fiancé.

Maybe he couldn't help himself and he killed the women he loved.

What if he became obsessed with her? A chill ran up her spine at the thought. She really needed to stop watching Lifetime TV.

Millie forced herself to try a few bites of chocolate covered bacon and a chocolate chunk brownie before heading back to the cabin. The chocolate made her feel slightly better and she patted her pocket. She had packed a few peanut butter chocolate bars in her pocket in case of an emergency.

Chapter 15

Millie tossed and turned all night. She couldn't shake the feeling that something was crawling around by her feet, but every time she checked, there was nothing there.

She woke abruptly to the sounds of soft snores coming from the upper bunk. It was dark, which made it hard to tell if it was the middle of the night or the middle of the day.

She stumbled out of bed and crept across the room to the bathroom. The worst part of having a roommate was trying to be stealthy.

In the bathroom, she turned on the faucet, filled her hands with cold water and splashed it on her face. After she finished brushing her teeth, she pulled on a pair of yellow capris and a sleeveless cotton blouse. She gave her gray locks a quick run through with the comb and pulled them back into a tight bun before flipping the light switch off.

Millie eased the door open. Sarah was wide-awake and sitting upright in bed, the TV remote in her hand as she flipped through the channels. "Where are you sneaking off to so early?"

Sarah hopped off the top bunk and landed on the floor with a thud. "Let me guess...you're going sleuthing."

"How did you know?"

Sarah reached around the side of Millie and grabbed her work clothes before heading to the bathroom. "Don't forget your secret suspect list." She winked and then stepped into the bathroom, quietly closing the door behind her.

Millie scowled. *How did Sarah know about the secret suspect list?* Even Annette hadn't seen the list.

She grabbed her backpack, loaded it with the important stuff - bottled water, her phone, her passport, some cash and last, but not least, the list, which she had tucked under the edge of her mattress.

Millie lifted the mattress and stuck her hand underneath. Her fingers ran over the cheap metal springs until they touched the small slip of paper.

She was running behind schedule and envisioned Annette standing near the gangway, champing at the bit.

Millie's guess wasn't too far off. She wasn't exactly champing - more like pacing back and forth. She waited until Annette had made another turn before stepping into sight. "I thought you were standing me up. You know, chickening out."

"I'm sorry. I'm running behind."

Annette grabbed a ball cap from her bag and pulled it low over her mop of dark hair. Next, she slipped on a pair of dark sunglasses.

She looked at Millie. "You're going like that? You'll stand out like a sore thumb." Annette reached inside her backpack and pulled out a matching cap. She gave it a quick snap and then stuck it on Millie's head.

Annette gave a small nod of satisfaction. "Let's go."

The women headed down the long dock and through a narrow gate, surrounded by a tall, chain link fence. Two armed guards stood near the exit.

Millie's brows drew together. "Is this a safe area?"

Annette quickened her pace. "I've heard this and that about some riff raff," she admitted. She came to an abrupt halt on the other side of the fence.

Up ahead, Millie could see several men milling about, lounging against the fence, looking in their direction...with a great deal of interest.

The hair on the back of Millie's neck stood up and she swallowed hard. They looked like a rough bunch. Ones that could easily take on two grandmotherly women.

Millie had lived her entire life in a nice, safe, mid-size town, but she watched the news and knew there were thugs on almost every street corner. On top of that, they were in a third world country.

Annette noted the look of concern on her friend's face. She dropped her backpack and reached inside. "Here. Take this." She shoved a small, silver whistle into Millie's hand.

"What do I do with this?"

"Blow the dang thing if you feel threatened."

Millie stared at the whistle in her hand. *And who would come if she blew it? More thugs?* She shook her head, but draped the dangling whistle around her neck since Annette had gone to all of the trouble of packing it.

Annette wasn't done. She pulled a round baton from her bag, zipped the backpack and stood upright. With a flick of her wrist, the metal baton doubled in size.

Millie frowned. It didn't look like a super scary weapon, but at least it appeared more effective than a whistle.

Annette slung her backpack over her shoulders. "Let's roll."

Millie drew her lips in a straight line. She had taken a self-defense class years ago at Roger's urging. One of the things she remembered the instructor telling the class was to walk with confidence, to hold your head high and if you feel threatened by someone, look them straight in the eye.

She did exactly that, as much out of fear, as wanting to remember what the person who was going to attack her looked like. The women made it over the bridge and just steps away from the small touristy area. They were almost home free.

From out of nowhere, a man vaulted over the low shrub and landed directly in front of them.

Tied across the man's face was a red bandanna. It reminded Millie of a stagecoach robber in an old Western movie. The only thing visible was the top of his head and his eyes, which were beady and dark.

He held a small knife in his hand and the blade was pointing right at Millie. "Give me your bag," he demanded.

Millie was not about to be stabbed over a stupid bag with twenty dollars and her cell phone inside. She lifted one side off her shoulder.

"I don't think so." Annette took a step back, raised her right leg and with as much force as she could muster, kicked the would-be thief squarely in the groin.

The man dropped to his knees and clutched his lower extremities. He fell to the ground and curled up in a ball. "Augh…"

"Take that, you loser." Annette grabbed Millie's arm and sidestepped the would-be thief. "C'mon."

Millie was not going to wait around to see what happened. She picked up the pace and fell in step with Annette. "That was awfully brave of you."

"Girl, I grew up in the hood. Ain't no little punk going to take me down," she told her. "Three or four? Now that's a different story."

The girls stopped in what had to be the center of the marketplace. Millie shaded her eyes and stared at the dilapidated buildings. The place wasn't much to look at. There were a few t-shirt shops, a small drugstore and a couple bars. Next to the drugstore was *Kingston Pet Store*.

Millie grabbed Annette's arm. "There it is."

They headed toward the small, nondescript clapboard building with peeling paint. Annette opened the door and Millie followed her inside where a blast of cool air greeted them.

The day was turning into a scorcher and the air-conditioned space was a welcome relief from the heat.

The interior looked even smaller than the outside. Shelves covered every inch of space. They were crammed full of fish food, dog collars, fish tanks and any other thing you might possibly need for your pet.

In the corner hung a large metal cage. Inside the cage was a bright red macaw, his tail feathers a brilliant shade of cobalt blue. Millie approached the cage. "Aren't you a pretty thing?"

"Aren't you a pretty thing," the bird mimicked.

Millie smiled and glanced at the nametag fastened to the bottom of the cage. "So your name is Winston."

"My name is Winston," the bird replied.

Annette wandered over. She had never seen a macaw up close. The bird tilted his head and eyed Annette. "Pretty lady."

Annette patted her hair. "Smart bird."

A man wearing a colorful knit cap that covered long, dark braided locks stepped out from the back. "He is for sale."

Annette shook her head. "I might be tempted, but the cruise ship won't let him on board."

"Ah, I see." He eyed the ship ID tags hanging around their neck.

"So you are not looking for a pet."

Millie shook her head. "No, but we were wondering if you may remember someone that came in recently to buy a spider. An envielous spider to be exact."

The tall man rested his elbows on the counter and dropped his chin in his hands. "Could be. I don't sell too many, although 'tis easy to find spiders on the island even when you don't want to," he joked.

"I may have sold one to a man not long ago," he added. "Of course, my memory is a little vague."

Millie unzipped the front compartment of her backpack and pulled out a five-dollar bill. She slid it across the counter. "Does this help?"

The man grabbed the bill and shoved it into his pocket. "It twas about a week ago."

Annette leaned against the counter. "Do you know what he looked like?"

The man rubbed his forehead. "Vaguely. Again, my memory. It's a little fuzzy."

Millie sighed and reached for another five. "Is it getting any clearer?"

He stuffed the bill in his pocket. "Yes. He was a tall man." He pointed to their tags. "He wore a tag like yours."

Annette rubbed her hands together. "Can you describe him?"

"He was a tall white man." He shrugged. "They all look the same to me."

Millie reached for her phone. She scrolled through the screen until she found the picture of Andy. "Is this the man who came in?"

The man squinted his eyes and studied the picture. "It could be."

She groaned and pulled another five from her purse. "Now does it look like the man?"

He grabbed the five and shoved it in his pocket. "Like I said, it could be. I'm not a hundred percent positive."

Millie slapped her forehead. "It could be" was not conclusive. The women thanked him for his time and headed out the door.

They stopped on the stoop. Annette turned back and glanced at the closed door. "What do you think?"

"That maybe Andy paid him off to buy his silence. I mean, it was either Andy or it wasn't."

They stopped inside the drugstore to buy a soda before starting the walk back to the ship. Millie spied the man they had had a run in with earlier.

He was hanging out on the corner - on the opposite side of the street.

When he saw them, he turned his back.

Annette nodded. "See? Gotta show 'em that we're not afraid. Otherwise, you're an easy target. So what about the sting? We might as well move onto phase two - the stakeout."

Millie had to agree. They would need to step up the investigation if they were ever going to figure out who killed Olivia.

"We need to spread the word that you have some kind of evidence hidden in your cabin."

Millie nodded. "Right. We need a gossip. Someone who can spread the word so-to-speak."

Annette snapped her fingers. "I've got just the person – Cat."

***

"...and one of the other crewmembers gave me a note that Olivia had written to them." Millie's eyes widened. She leaned close to Cat, who was on the other side of the counter. "She said that if anything happened to her, this person was a prime suspect."

Cat pulled the number two pencil from her hair and began chewing on the end. "Who was it?"

"I can't say. It might put my own life in danger." She drummed her fingertips on the glass display case. "I'm waiting for Dave Patterson to get back on board later tonight. I'm gonna take the note to him, but for now, it's safe and sound inside my cabin." She winked at Cat and then glanced at her watch. "I better go. Trivia starts in ten minutes."

She could feel the heat on the back of her head as Cat's eyes bore into her skull. *I should get an academy award for that performance,* Millie decided.

Annette was waiting for her near the bank of elevators. "Did you do it?"

"Mission accomplished."

The girls made a quick trip to Millie's cabin where Annette removed the bathroom ceiling panel.

Millie helped push her up and into the space. "Are you sure about this?" Visions of Annette becoming trapped in the ceiling and suffocating filled her head. If anything happened to Annette, Millie would be in hot water, not to mention the loss of a good friend.

"Nah. I'm fine. This is a piece of cake."

Millie watched as Annette crawled over to the open vent and she waited to make sure Annette was in the right spot. "Do you have your phone?"

Annette flashed her cell phone through the vent. "Check."

"I'll be back as soon as trivia is over." Millie didn't wait for her friend to reply. She left the cabin door ajar and headed up to deck seven to start trivia.

Thankfully, Sarah had gone ashore with her friend, Nikki, for the day. Now all they had to do was wait and hope that Cat *would* spread the word in time.

The trivia game was all about food, and the questions were easy, at least to Millie.

Since it was a port day, there were only a handful of participants. It was still fun and there were several winners who walked away with the dime store trophies – a gold colored palm tree glued to a small plastic platform. Blazoned across the front in bold, gold letters, was the ship's name, the *Siren of the Seas*.

Millie shoved the folder back in the cabinet and locked the door. She made a quick stop by the crew mess for a plate of some unrecognizable stew concoction and a scoop of rice. She ate alone and watched as several other crewmembers wandered in and out.

She had just finished eating when her cell phone beeped. She pulled it from her pocket and glanced at the screen. It was a message from Annette, "Mission accomplished."

Millie tossed her dirty plates in the bin near the door and darted out of the room.

Annette was pacing the cabin floor when Millie arrived. "You're never gonna believe who just snuck into your cabin."

Chapter 16

"But how can that be? All of the clues lead right to Andy." First, there was the receipt Millie had found in his medicine cabinet. The man at the pet store told them a man had bought the spider - not a woman. Then there was the matter of Andy's deceased fiancé, not that that was proof that he killed Olivia.

On the one hand, Millie was greatly relieved it wasn't Andy who snuck into her cabin in search of the non-existent note.

Could it be that perhaps he and the person Annette spotted sneaking into the cabin were in cahoots? Maybe together, they had hatched a plan to kill the poor girl.

It was time to pay another visit to Dave Patterson's office.

Annette looked down at her dusty clothes and then glanced at her watch. "I gotta go change and head back to the kitchen." She handed her cell phone to Millie. "Take this down to Patterson."

"He'll probably want to keep it," Millie warned.

"Yeah, I know. Maybe he can figure out how to transfer the video to his computer."

Millie raised a brow. That was a great idea. Annette had some great ideas. Millie decided right then and there that her friend was the perfect sleuthing partner.

She watched Annette traipse down the hall before closing the cabin door and heading to the bathroom to wash up. The hot, humid tropics made her normally straight, smooth locks zing straight out from her head.

Millie wet her comb and ran it through her hair. Next, she spritzed some hairspray and then patted her hair down.

Satisfied with the results, she wandered out of the bathroom and checked her appearance in the full-length mirror. It wouldn't be long before the passengers returned to the ship tired, hot and hungry.

Millie found Andy near the main gangplank. He was chatting with Detective Patterson, who nodded to her when she got close. "I heard you and your sidekick, Annette, were in town today, snooping around."

"You could call it that."

Patterson crossed his arms and rocked back on his heels. "And?"

"I have some new information. Can I stop by your place later?"

"Of course." He nodded to Andy before heading across the room and disappearing into an elevator.

Andy rubbed a hand across his bushy brow. "You're not gonna let this go, are you?"

Millie swallowed hard. "I can't. I think I know who the killer - or should I say - killers are."

Andy didn't have a chance to reply. A young couple stumbled over the threshold. The man swayed back and forth.

"Whoa there pardner. Let's get you two back to your room." Andy looked at Millie over the top of the man's head. "I'll be back in a flash."

Millie nodded and then turned her attention to the next round of guests coming up the gangplank.

The rest of the afternoon sailed by as Millie and Andy greeted the returning guests like family. Many of the faces were beginning to look familiar.

Several of the guests that stopped to chat were from Millie's trivia games and they greeted her by name.

228

Andy shifted his feet. "You're popular with the passengers."

"Just doing my job," she shot back.

After the last passenger had boarded, the crew pulled the gangplank and closed the door.

Andy turned to Millie. "Tonight is formal night."

Millie nodded as she remembered the time Roger and she had dressed up on their cruise's formal night. The picture - one of the last pictures they had taken together - used to hang in the living room, above the fireplace.

After the divorce, in a fit of anger, Millie had almost shredded the picture. At the last minute, she changed her mind. Someday, she would give the portrait to her daughter, Beth.

The thought of her home caused her to feel the teensiest bit homesick. The feeling quickly passed, though, as she remembered she needed to stop by

Detective Patterson's office before she started her evening shift.

"You'll need to make an appearance at the past guest party," Andy told her. "That's where they formally introduce the crew to the passengers."

"Are you hosting it?"

Andy nodded. "Yep. Truth be told, it's one of my favorite events. I love the excitement the past guests bring with them. Return guests - they're the best passengers in the world."

Millie had to agree. The greatest compliment one could receive was people who loved the ship, the staff and kept coming back for more.

"I'll meet you backstage at five o'clock." The party started at 5:30 – forty-five minutes before the first seating dinner.

Millie patted her pocket to make sure she still had Annette's phone before making her way to Dave Patterson's office.

"Come in."

Patterson was seated at his desk and he waved Millie inside.

He leaned back as she pulled out the chair and perched on the edge. Her underarms immediately started to perspire. She wished more than anything that the man didn't make her so nervous.

"Did you enjoy your day in Jamaica?"

Millie nodded. Then she thought of the would-be robber. "We were almost robbed," she blurted out.

"You were?"

"Yeah." Millie rubbed her damp palms across the top of her pants. "Annette. Annette Delacroix knows a few self-defense moves and took the would-be robber down. Literally."

"You don't say."

"She kicked him in the groin area."

Patterson chuckled. "Sounds like Annette. You gotta watch her, especially if she gets fired up and happens to be in the kitchen holding a knife."

Millie smiled nervously.

"So what brings you to my office?" he asked.

She pulled Annette's cell phone from her front pocket and laid it on the desk. "Before you look at this, let me tell you what I know so far."

Millie told him about how Annette and she had gone to the pet store in Kingston and they discovered that an employee on their ship had purchased a small terrarium, complete with a rare envielous spider.

She also told him how Annette and she had spread the word that she had evidence in her cabin.

Dave leaned forward. "How did you plan on the suspect entering your cabin?"

"We left the door ajar."

"Did anyone show up?"

Millie nodded. "We caught her on camera."

Dave grabbed Annette's cell phone, scrolled to the video and pressed play. "How did you get this videotape?"

"Annette. She...it was taken from the ceiling vent in my cabin."

"Annette Delacroix was in your ceiling?"

"Yes. She popped the access panel in the bathroom ceiling and crawled across until she reached the vent that looks down on the main part of the cabin."

Dave Patterson had heard it all. "You're kidding."

"She's pretty wiry," Millie said.

Patterson studied the video. "This is definitely incriminating evidence."

He continued. "I'll bring Cat in for questioning, but that doesn't make her the killer," he pointed out.

"Maybe an accessory?"

"The store owner couldn't positively identify anyone. Are you sure he's not lying and it was a woman who bought the terrarium and spider?"

Millie shrugged. Nothing was certain. If she had to choose between Andy and Cat being the guilty party, she would have to go with Cat, not that she *wished* Cat were the killer. Her first choice would be someone she didn't know.

Patterson stood.

Millie took it as her signal that the meeting had ended. She scrambled to her feet and sidestepped the chair as she made her way to the door.

"I'll let you know if anything comes from my conversation with Cat," Patterson promised as he held the door for Millie.

Patterson shook his head and slowly closed the door. Annette Delacroix? Now that was another story.

***

Millie's stomach began to churn. She didn't want to believe Andy was involved. He just didn't seem like the killer-type. Maybe she wasn't the great judge of character that she always thought she was.

She tried to put herself in Roger's shoes. What would he do? Try to squeeze out a confession? Catch the killer in a trap? The girls had already done the stakeout - technically.

Back in the cabin, she pulled her list of suspects from her backpack. Number one on the list was

Andy. Number two - Maribelle. Cat was on the list but further down. Millie moved her to the top, above Andy.

There was something missing...a small niggle that didn't add up. She glanced at her watch. It would have to wait until later. It was time to head down to the past guest party.

Chapter 17

Millie glanced nervously from behind the curtain as she peeked into the theater. It was filling up fast. Andy stood nearby, talking to the magician. He gave Millie a reassuring smile when he caught her eye.

He strolled over to where Millie was peeking around the edge of the curtain. "There are a lot of people in there," she whispered furiously. If she thought her stomach was churning earlier, it was now doing a few somersaults.

Andy detected the hint of panic in her voice. He placed a reassuring arm around her shoulders and gave her a gentle hug. "Don't worry. You'll do just fine."

Millie attempted a half-hearted smile before turning her attention to the gathering crowd.

By the time Andy took the stage, Millie was starting to feel woozy.

Zack walked by and noticed the white, drawn look on Millie's face. He reached into his pocket and pulled out a mint. "Here. This will settle your stomach," he told her.

"Thank you." Millie gratefully accepted the mint. She pulled it from the wrapper and popped it into her mouth.

Just then, she heard Andy announce her name. "And now to introduce the one, the only, my new assistant and sidekick, Millie."

Horrified, Millie attempted to swallow the barely eaten mint. It made it halfway down before lodging in her throat. She began to gag. The mint, like a mini missile, flew out of her mouth.

She jerked her hand and caught it mid-air, quickly shoving the wet disc into her pocket before plastering a terrified smile on her face and stepping out from behind the curtain.

Andy met her halfway across the stage. He gave her a reassuring nudge forward and handed her a microphone.

"This is Millie's first week on board, folks," Andy told the packed theater. "How do you think she's doing?"

A round of thunderous applause ensued. Millie thought she even caught a few catcalls. Her face turned bright red...the same color as the tip of the microphone.

Millie held the microphone to her mouth. "Thank you. Thank you, everyone." Her eyes scanned the crowd. People were smiling at her. She felt herself relax - just a little.

"You. The passengers...make my job easy. You all are so much fun. Thank you for making my first week one of the best weeks of my life," she finished sincerely.

Before Andy could put her on the spot again, she shut the microphone off and handed it to him. She turned on her heel and exited stage left, waving to her adoring fans as she walked.

Back behind the curtain, she slumped against the wall, pulled the tacky mint from her pocket and stuck it back in her mouth.

Zack patted Millie's shoulder. "You did great."

The dancers were lining up behind the curtain for their performance. She gave him a weak smile and thumbs up before she headed down the stairs and into the dressing room to wait for Andy.

While she waited, Millie had a sudden thought. It was something she should have considered before. She couldn't wait for Andy to be done - to ask him one simple question. Her mind raced at how to pose the question without raising too much suspicion.

She didn't have to wait long. Andy appeared around the corner. His face was flushed, his eyes bright with excitement. "You did great. The crowd loves you."

Millie smiled. It felt good, now that her stage fright had subsided. "Thanks."

"Let's go back to my cabin. I have something for you," he said.

Millie followed him out of the dressing room and down to the lower deck. He unlocked his cabin door and swung it wide, letting Millie step inside first.

Millie glanced around. This was perfect. It was better than what she could have imagined. The feeling quickly faded as Andy reached into his cabinet, pulled out a wrapped package and handed it to Millie.

Andy was giving her a gift.

Guilt consumed her. How could she have ever suspected Andy was a killer?

"You have a great cabin," she told Andy as she looked around.

He nodded. "I almost feel guilty with all of this extra space."

"Even your bathroom. The luxury of having two large medicine cabinets." She set the package on the table, wandered over to the bathroom and opened the door. "Why look at all this room."

She stepped inside. "You even have medicine cabinets." She opened the cabinet door on the right. It was full of men's grooming supplies. "Just look at all of this shelf space."

Millie prayed she wasn't crossing the line and that Andy wouldn't wonder what on earth she was doing.

She opened the cabinet on the opposite side, the one with the wallet and receipt inside. "And you don't even use this other one."

"No," he shook his head. "The other cabinet belonged to Toby, your predecessor."

Millie reached for the wallet, still tucked under the edge. It was right where she had left it. She picked it up and held it out. "Oh, there's something in here. It looks like a wallet." She held it up for Andy to see.

"Hmm. That doesn't belong to me. Toby must've forgotten it."

He picked it up and turned it over in his hand. "Yes, it's his. He must've forgotten it." Andy tapped the top. "Those are his initials."

Millie's heart skipped a beat as she slipped her reading glasses on and stared at the leather exterior. She hadn't noticed the lettering before. *"TDO."*

"Tobias D. Oglesby." Andy said. "I should send it to him."

"You might want to give that to Detective Patterson."

Andy's head shot up and he stared at Millie. "Why is that?"

She took the wallet from Andy, opened it up and stuck her finger inside one of the compartments...the one with the receipt. She pulled the receipt out and handed it to Andy.

He unfolded it. "You knew this was inside?"

"Yes."

"Why didn't you take it to Detective Patterson?"

Millie wasn't quite sure why she hadn't. Maybe she had panicked or maybe she hadn't wanted to believe Andy was capable of murder.

Either way, she should have given it to him or at the very least, told him about it. Hopefully, she wouldn't get into too much trouble. "Deep down I couldn't believe you were the killer."

Andy started for the door and abruptly halted. "Wait. You forgot your gift." He reached over and grabbed the present.

Millie turned the package over, slipped her finger under the tape, and gently lifted. She pulled the paper off and set the box on the table. Tucked inside was a large, silver flashlight.

She lifted it from the box and turned it over in her hand. "This flashlight weighs a ton." *Was Andy going to put her on some sort of night patrol as punishment?*

"This isn't just any old flashlight, Millie." He turned it over so that the bottom was facing up. "It's part flashlight, part Taser."

Millie's eyes widened. She had never seen a real Taser.

"I'll show you how to use it."

"I-I don't know what to say other than this is the most interesting gift I've ever gotten."

Andy handed it back. "Now you can be safe no matter where you are. Let's head to Patterson's office."

"Cat and Toby - were they friends?" Millie asked Andy as they walked.

He shook his head. "I'm not sure. They had kind of an odd relationship, those two. There was some sort of connection but I'm not sure what it was."

Luckily, Patterson was in his office. He raised a brow when he saw the two of them walk in together.

Andy placed the wallet on the desk and explained how Millie found the receipt inside and that it had belonged to Toby.

Dave listened quietly before turning to Millie. "You never told me about this? I'll deal with you later," he added ominously. "Cat Wellington is on her way down now."

Millie reached for the door handle. "I'd rather she not see me."

"Yeah, we should get out of here," Andy added.

Millie and her boss strolled to the bank of elevators, and Andy waited while Millie stepped in first. She didn't dare mention her aversion to elevators, certain that he already thought she had plenty of quirks without adding another to the growing list.

The door started to close. Just before it shut, she caught a glimpse of Cat walking toward Detective Patterson's office.

***

Millie was on pins and needles the rest of the evening and all through the night as she wondered what happened when Patterson questioned Cat.

She didn't have to wait long. Annette caught up with her in the crew mess hall early the next morning. "Cat's in the hoosegow."

Millie's mouth dropped open. "You mean Cat is in jail?"

Annette grabbed her arm and propelled her into the hall. "They're holding her 'til we get back to port and they can arrest Toby Oglesby for murder. Patterson suspects Cat was an accessory."

That made sense. Toby killed Olivia, escaped from the ship and for some reason, he left Cat behind to tidy up the loose ends.

Millie spent the rest of the day mulling over the events that had taken place. She had actually helped solve a murder, with Annette's help, of course.

Not far behind that, she was relieved Andy hadn't been involved.

The rest of the day was jam-packed with activities that kept Millie on her toes and on her feet, literally.

By the time evening rolled around, she was ready to collapse. Tomorrow was turnover day and from all that she'd been told, it was the busiest day of the week, trying to get all the departing guests off and a fresh, new crowd on.

She kneeled next to her bed that night. "Dear Heavenly Father. Thank you for a good week. Thank you for helping me make it through. Thank you for all of the new friends I've made and let me always shine Your light for others to see."

A Bible verse popped into her head: *"In the same way, let your light shine before others, that they may see your good deeds and glorify your Father in heaven."* Matthew 5:16 NIV

She finished her prayers and climbed into bed. Millie was out like a light as soon as her head touched the pillow.

Chapter 18

BEEP...BEEP. Sarah groaned and Millie buried her head in her pillow as the alarm went off early the next morning.

"You go first," Sarah said as she pulled the covers over her head and sunk down.

Millie sighed as she shoved her feet in her slippers and shuffled to the bathroom. The bright bathroom light blinded her and Millie closed her eyes as she waited for her eyes to adjust.

By the time she showered and dressed, she felt much better. She couldn't wait to find out what happened to Toby - and Cat.

Andy was already on deck five when she arrived. The line of passengers waiting to disembark started at the exit door, snaked around the atrium and down the hall. The line stretched as far as the eye could see.

Millie smiled and waved to some of the familiar faces as the two of them made their way to the exit, just as the crew opened the door and the first passengers started to disembark.

She kept the smile on her face until the very last passenger exited the ship and the security guard stationed near the exit nodded to Andy. "Last one," he announced.

Andy's shoulders sagged and he glanced at his watch. "Another one bites the dust," he said. "You have a few hours of downtime, Millie, if you'd like to go ashore."

Millie decided she could use a few personal items like aspirin and sunscreen - items they sold on board the ship but for a lot more money than what she could buy them for in Miami.

She ran down to her cabin and grabbed her wallet. She shoved that and her cell phone in her backpack and headed for the exit.

Millie switched her phone on as soon as she cleared the ship. There was a message from her daughter, Beth. "Hi, Mom. I called to find out how you liked your first week on board the ship."

She blinked back tears at the sound of her daughter's voice. Millie erased the message and then dialed Beth's number before heading to a shady spot to talk.

Beth picked up on the first ring. "So how was it?"

"Exciting. Busy. Tiring."

"Did you make any friends?" her daughter asked.

Millie grinned. "Yep."

"And a few enemies," she added.

"Enemies?"

"There was a murder on board the ship I helped solve and in the process I guess I stepped on a few toes."

Beth laughed. "You're beginning to sound like Gloria."

That sounded like a compliment to Millie. "Gloria" was Gloria Rutherford, Millie's cousin. She lived in a small town not far from Millie's place. Over the past couple of years, Gloria had developed a reputation for solving mysteries.

"It must run in the family," Millie said proudly. She had almost forgotten about her cousin and her recent notoriety. She made a mental note to give Gloria a call so that they could compare notes.

Beth and Millie talked for a bit longer and Millie was sad when the conversation finally ended. She promised to give her daughter a call the next week and in turn, Beth promised to give her brother,

Blake, a call to let him know their mother was safe and happy.

Millie ran her few errands. It was nice to be off the ship and on American soil, a place where she felt relatively safe walking around on her own.

She loaded her backpack with the toiletries, some snacks she decided she couldn't live without and a couple books she was looking forward to reading.

She made a mental note to run by the library the next time they were in port so she could check out some books and read them in her free time. Now that Olivia's murder investigation had ended, Millie hoped things would settle down.

She slipped her sunglasses on and quickened her pace as she headed back to the ship.

Millie joined the back of the line where several other crewmembers were waiting to board. Her eyes widened when she spied Cat and Dave Patterson boarding just ahead of her. She ducked behind another crewmember in an attempt to hide, but it was too late.

It was as if Cat could sense Millie was behind her. She narrowed her eyes and glared at Millie.

Dave Patterson noticed her, too. She watched him board and stand off to the side, as if waiting for someone, which he was...Millie. "I trust you enjoyed your day off."

Millie nodded and patted her backpack. "Stocking up on the necessities."

He nodded. "Do you have a minute?"

"Yes. Of course."

"Follow me."

Millie followed him down the hall and to his office. He unlocked the door and waited for Millie to enter first. "Have a seat," he told her.

Millie picked the chair closest to the door and perched on the edge. Her armpits began to sweat, an all too familiar occurrence whenever she was close to Dave Patterson. She began to squirm under his intense gaze.

"Toby Oglesby confessed to Olivia's murder," he announced.

Patterson watched as Millie nervously fiddled with the zipper on her backpack. "I'm glad to hear that."

"I bet you're wondering how Catherine Wellington was involved."

"I am a bit curious."

"Cat and Toby's mother are best friends. Close, almost like sisters. Cat was the one who got Toby the job on board the ship. Cat also knew that Toby was fixated on Olivia."

Patterson explained that Toby hung around the store almost every day, trying to talk to Olivia, who blew him off.

Toby had a bit of a temper and when it started to sink in that Olivia was not going to give him the time of the day, he got angry...angry enough to hint to Cat that something bad might happen to Olivia.

When Olivia died, Cat immediately became suspicious that Toby may have somehow been involved. She had nothing concrete - just her suspicions.

"And when Cat heard you had some kind of note that Olivia had written, she panicked. She wanted to take a look at the note before you turned it over to the authorities in case it implicated Toby," he finished.

"But wouldn't that make her an accessory, or at the very least tampering with a police investigation?"

Patterson leaned forward, his hands resting on the desk. "It might have except for the fact that you didn't have a note. It never existed, so there's nothing to charge her with. Plus, she claims she only wanted to look at the note, not take it," he pointed out. "Toby said he never confessed the murder to his mother or Cat."

Millie's brow furrowed. That part was probably true. After all, Toby was off the ship right after they discovered Olivia's body on the atrium floor. "So now what?" she asked.

"Toby has been arrested." Dave Patterson wasn't finished. "You're lucky I don't turn you in for withholding evidence."

Millie's heart skipped a beat. She knew she should have turned the receipt over to Patterson as soon as she discovered it. "I won't let it happen again," she promised.

He abruptly stood. "This is your warning. Next time I won't be quite so forgiving," he said somberly.

Patterson walked her to the door and his expression softened. "Now try to stay out of trouble."

Millie gave a small salute. "I'll do my best, sir." She stepped out into the hall and started down the long corridor.

Millie smiled and picked up the pace as she headed to her cabin. Today had been a great day. She had solved her first mystery and still had a job - at least for another week.

The end.

If you enjoyed reading "Starboard Secrets," would you please take a moment to leave a review? It would mean so much to me. Thank you! - Hope Callaghan

The Series Continues with Book 2, "Portside Peril"

Books in This Series

Starboard Secrets: Book 1
Portside Peril: Book 2
Lethal Lobster: Book 3
Deadly Deception: Book 4
Vanishing Vacationers: Book 5
Cruise Control: Book 6
Killer Karaoke: Book 7
Suite Revenge: Book 8
Cruisin' for a Bruisin': Book 9
High Seas Heist: Book 10
Family, Friends and Foes: Book 11
Murder on Main: Book 12
Fatal Flirtation: Book 13
Deadly Delivery: Book 14
Reindeer & Robberies: Book 15
Transatlantic Tragedy: Book 16
Southampton Stalker: Book 17
Book 18: Coming Soon!
Cruise Ship Mysteries Box Set I (Books 1-3)
Cruise Ship Mysteries Box Set II (Books 4-6)
Cruise Ship Mysteries Box Set III (Books 7-9)
Cruise Ship Mysteries Box Set IV (Books 10-12)

Get New Releases & More

Get New Releases, Giveaways & Discounted Books When You Subscribe To My Free Cozy Mysteries Newsletter!

hopecallaghan.com/newsletter

Meet Author Hope Callaghan

Hope loves to connect with her readers! Connect with her today!

Never miss another book deal! Text the word Books to 33222

Visit **hopecallaghan.com/newsletter** for
special offers, free books,
and soon-to-be-released books!

Facebook:
facebook.com/authorhopecallaghan/
Amazon:
amazon.com/Hope-Callaghan/e/B00OJ5X702
Pinterest:
pinterest.com/cozymysteriesauthor/

Hope Callaghan is an American author who loves to write clean fiction books, especially Christian

Mystery and Cozy Mystery books. <u>She has written more than 70 mystery books (and counting)</u> in six series.

In March 2017, Hope won a Mom's Choice Award for her book, <u>"Key to Savannah,"</u> Book 1 in the Made in Savannah Cozy Mystery Series.

Born and raised in a small town in West Michigan, she now lives in Florida with her husband. She is the proud mother of 3 wonderful children.

When she's not doing the thing she loves best - writing books - she enjoys cooking, traveling and reading books.

Apple Crisp Recipe

Ingredients

4 cups sliced apples (about 4 medium)

2/3 cup packed light brown sugar

½ cup all-purpose flour

½ cup quick oats (can substitute w/graham cracker crumbs)

¾ tsp. ground cinnamon

¾ tsp. nutmeg

1/3 cup butter, softened

Heat oven to 375 degrees. Arrange apples in greased glass baking dish (8x8).

Mix sugar, flour, oats, cinnamon and nutmeg until blended. Add butter. Blend until mixture sticks together.

Sprinkle mixture over apples.

Bake uncovered 25 – 30 minutes (until topping is brown and firm).

Serve warm with vanilla ice cream.

*This recipe also works well with mixed berries (strawberries, blueberries, raspberries & blackberries).

Made in the USA
Middletown, DE
09 June 2023

32286434R00161